# The Alpha Pair

Nicole Rivers

To every author
who helped me never forget:
Romance is better with magic…
And spice.

# CHAPTER ONE

## *Hope*

The moon's call was igniting a fire in my blood. I could almost feel the breeze ruffling my fur as I made my way to the forest. My wolf loved running, but when it was a full moon? I could barely convince her to shift back to my human side. Taking a deep breath and walking deeper into the trees behind my house, I scanned the shadows for anyone who might see me. As soon as I established my solitude, I shifted and took off.

Outrunning your demons was a lot easier when you were a wolf.

The wind brushed through my fur, cooling me down even as my wolf pushed herself harder, faster. She loved getting out as often as possible, although it meant avoiding everyone but my sister. Wolves may be pack animals, but that's only if they're accepted by the pack. My father had made damn sure that mine was rejected.

"No one wants a runty bitch," his voice was like a nightmare on repeat. "Especially not me. Keep that nasty wolf to yourself," the venom in his voice haunted me even years later.

My wolf shook her head, clearing the thoughts as she ran even faster. By the time we made it to the stream, we were exhausted. It would have to be an easy jog back to the house.

Ugh. The house.

Dad would hopefully be passed out, or just not home at all. He seemed to be on edge the last few days, lashing out at Briana and I more than normal. I'd avoided most of it; I was a lot faster than I had been as a kid, but he'd managed to get a swipe in. It had finally faded this morning, the skin on the back of my neck only a slight pink.

I shifted back and began pulling on the clothes I'd left in the hollow of my favorite pine. Patting the bark, I imagined myself putting on my armor. You don't survive in a house like mine without it.

The walk back seemed to end in a heartbeat, but that was how it always was. Any relief I found in the woods was quickly beaten back by this house. Or literally beat back by the asshole known as my father.

I gently opened the front door, easing inside right before it creaked. It was quiet, but the heaviness, the tension, told me that he was home. Barely suppressing a sigh, I made my way to the kitchen for a snack.

Grabbing a banana, I tried to make my way down the

hallway undetected. The show he had playing could mask the sounds if I was lucky.

"Hope, get in here!"

Or not. Dammit. I gathered myself, taking a deep breath in as I made my way into the living room.

"Yes?" If my voice stayed neutral, it helped. Sometimes.

"Where the fuck have you been? I've been looking everywhere for you." His bloodshot eyes told a different story.

"I just stepped outside for a little bit, tha-"

"Outside?" Shit. I did not think that part through.

"Yep, just wanted to check on some plants. You know how they get when it's this hot.." I was rambling.

"You sure you weren't out there turning into that little shit of a wolf?" My wolf raged at that. Just one more year, I thought. One more year and I could take Bri away from this hellhole without getting arrested for kidnapping.

"Nope. I know your rules," I said, keeping my eyes downcast. Hiding the anger in them was becoming more and more impossible.

"Bullshit," he spat, stumbling to his feet. "But it doesn't matter now. You're about to be someone else's problem."

My stomach churned at the veiled threat. Had he finally

found some way to get rid of me?

"What do you mean?" I asked, my neutral tone wavering. He took a step forward, swaying on his feet.

"The alpha and I spoke, you're going to mate. It's all worked out, he's announcing it at the All Pack meeting next week."

I could not have heard him right. The alpha? He was thirty years older than me and a walking domestic violence ad.

"What the fuck? No, we're not," I said, the words spilling out before I could stop them.

"What did you just say?" He stepped forward again, the smell of whiskey and body odor threatening to make me lose the few bites of banana I'd managed.

Years of biting my tongue, of trying to not get kicked out so Bri wouldn't be alone, came crashing down.

"Sorry, let me be more clear," I raised my eyes to his, jutting my chin out. "There is no way in hell that I am marrying that old, horrible, sexist piece of shit. I may have had to live with one abusive asshole, but I don't have a choice in who my father is. I sure as hell do when it comes to my mate."

He just stared at me, a small smile playing at his lips. I'd run from that smile for years, but not anymore.

Not now.

Not today.

"You little bitch." His voice was full of venom, causing my cheeks to sting. I took a step back, my body screaming at me to run. "You think just because you're grown you can talk to me like that? If you weren't about to be useful for the first time in your goddamn life, I'd kick you out."

Useful for the first time? God, I would laugh if I thought it would do anything other than piss him off. Only he would consider someone raising his other child, keeping the house from falling into absolute disarray and keeping everyone fed not "useful."

"Anthony is not my mate. I won't, nor will I ever, choose him." I kept my voice firm, my eyes locked on his.

"You don't have to. I did for you." Suddenly he was in my face, the smell making my eyes water now. How he moved so quickly while completely loaded would never make sense to me. "It'd be a shame if something happened to the alpha's mate before she even made it down the aisle," he stroked the side of my cheek with nails he had shifted into claws, then moved them down to my throat, pinching hard on either side.

I held my breath, refusing to give him the satisfaction of gasping. Just as little dots danced across my vision, he let go. I massaged my throat when he turned away, trying to calm my wolf. She wanted to tear him apart.

"Good thing I have a back up."

My blood turned to ice. Whatever argument I had died on my lips.

Bri.

He would do it. He would make her marry that disgusting old man as soon as she turned 18, not even caring that Anthony would probably add her to his list of murdered mates.

A lead weight settled on my chest. This was going to happen - either to me, or worse, to the one person I have tried to protect my entire life.

"Fine." I gritted out between clenched teeth.

"That's what I thought. Try to show some excitement at the meeting. Who wouldn't want to marry their alpha?" He sneered, his eyes already going back to his show.

Me. That's who.

# CHAPTER TWO

## *Hope*

The low chuckle behind me as I turned to leave left my ears, and stomach, burning with shame. I knew what I had to do and would sacrifice everything for Bri, but giving him any feelings of triumph felt... More than just wrong. It felt disgusting.

Pushing my way back outside, I paced over to the trees. The rough bark under my fingertips usually helped me calm down. I could come outside and find peace in these woods. Safety.

Having my future stolen seemed to have ruined that.

"Hope?"

I pasted a fake smile on my face, hoping Bri wouldn't notice. How had I not heard her walking up? God, I needed to be more alert.

"Hey, what's up?" I asked, attempting to sound as light as possible. I hoped the forced cheer would keep her from suspecting anything.

"What's wrong?" She asked, her worried eyes taking in my face.

Or not.

"Nothing, I'm fine. But I do need to talk to you about something."

"Why do you sound like somebody died?" She asked, the furrow in her brow deepening. My smile wavered as I fought down the urge to tell the truth. Nobody had died. Just my future.

Better mine than hers.

"Nobody died, Bri. It's not that bad. Dad had some... Things to share with me when I was home earlier. It looks like he's arranged my mating." I kept my voice neutral as I looked past her at the house.

"What?! He can't do that! No one does that anymore."

"That's not entirely true. The alpha's niece? Their wedding is this fall."

"Chelsea didn't ask for that shit and I'm not sure it's really going to happen."

Chelsea? "I didn't realize you two knew each other? Okay, it doesn't matter whether it happens or not anymore. It's happening for me." I took a breath, trying to soothe the rage that was hovering. "Dad and the Alpha worked it all out. He's telling everyone at the All Pack meeting."

"Wait... The Alpha? As in the dick who is old enough to be your FATHER? There's no way. You can't do that!"

"I am doing that. I know he's older, and kind of awful, but look at Mom and Dad. They were fated mates and he tortured her. It obviously doesn't matter how you come together, mating is just shit all the way around." The bitterness was bleeding out of me.

"Why would you agree to that? You don't have to do what he says, you can leave."

"And leave you behind? Seriously? That's not an option, we stay together. No matter what."

"Hope..." Her eyes started to water and her voice was shaking. "Did he.. Did he use me to threaten you?"

Shit. I was really hoping she would not figure that out. I moved to her, hugging her tight against me.

"Hey. It's okay, everything is okay. You don't need to worry. I will figure this out and we will be safe and together, okay? That's all that matters."

"You didn't answer my question," Her voice was muffled by my shoulder but I could still hear the irritation there.

"No, I didn't because it doesn't matter. Dad's the worst, okay. We know that. Hell, I think the whole pack knows it."

She gave a wet chuckle, pulling away.

"Do you want to go for a run and try to burn off some of this worry? We don't leave for the meeting until tomorrow and with how drunk Dad was earlier, I'd be surprised if he was still awake."

"Yeah, let's do it."

I smiled and walked deeper into the woods, relief flooding me. The hard part was over. At least, with my sister. The meeting with the Crescent River Pack was another story entirely. While our wolves took over, running through the humid air, my mind played out what the next week would look like.

The Alpha was bound to plan some grand reveal towards the end of the week. He didn't know how close I had been with the other pack's alpha, otherwise he would do it on the first day just to spite both of us.

The breeze cooled us as we made it to the spot next to the stream where we kept extra clothes. Shifting back and getting dressed, we laid in the afternoon sun, neither of us acknowledging that this could be the last time we would do this for a while. Potentially ever.

Most mates take their time, move in, get engaged and eventually have a mating ceremony that doubles as a wedding. Our alpha had already been married twice and both times, he had announced it and his future mate moved in within a few days. Both of his previous mates had also died.

The official word on that was natural causes. Anyone with

eyes and a brain knew he beat them to death.

"What are you going to do about Jensen?" Bri asked, breaking the silence.

"Uh.. Jensen? You mean the other pack's alpha?" I asked, attempting to cool the fire in my blood that hit whenever he was mentioned. God, this was ridiculous.

Bri rolled her eyes as she smiled at me. "Sure, let's act like that name means nothing to you. I'm not blind, Hope. I'm not sure what happened a few years ago, but I know how you two still respond to each other."

"We haven't even spoken to each other in years, let alone 'responded' to each other, whatever the hell that means."

I knew what that meant, at least for me. I could not see that man without feeling extremely pissed off. My wolf, on the other hand, still wanted to claim him. We were generally on the same page, but the All Pack meeting was a nightmare of her trying to shift and fuck around and me being pissed off and aloof.

Adding a surprise forced engagement to that should really make things... Super fun.

"It means you two gravitate towards each other. And if you actually get within a ten foot radius?" She asked, her smile widening, "You are both as stiff as a board and completely checked out."

"We are not completely checked out. There is no we! It was a long time ago that there was even a possibility of a we and now.. Well, last I heard he was engaged." I couldn't even finish the thought without the burning in my chest amping up. I cleared my throat, wrestling with the keening my wolf was giving off.

Bri's eyes changed, shifting to the yellow of her wolf. "I can… I can feel her. God, it feels like you've lost half of yourself. Is that what it always feels like?"

"It's not that bad. Please get out of my wolf's mind. Or feelings. Or whatever the fuck you are doing, please. Stop," I pleaded, doing everything I could to shut down the pain. Everyone has a first love when they're kids, but mine didn't seem to want to go away.

"I'm sorry, I don't mean to. Sometimes my wolf just can't help it. And the pain yours is projecting is trying to bring mine to her knees. If I can feel that, the alpha definitely will be able to. What are you going to do?" She questioned, her brows drawing together in worry.

"Avoid Jensen, get engaged, and survive," I said, poking her in the side. "We're Kelly girls. We always survive."

Her lips turned up for a second. She looked past me as her eyes turned back to their normal green. "Does this time feel different to you? I can't shake the feeling that something is coming." She shook her head and rolled her eyes. "Sorry, I'm sure I'm just imagining things."

"It's okay," I said, hoping she couldn't hear how my heart had sped up. I knew exactly what she was talking about and it terrified me.

# CHAPTER THREE

## *Hope*

The drive to the lake was uneventful and tense. My dad had driven Anthony, so it was just Bri and I. We didn't talk very much, both of us preoccupied with what was coming.

The All Pack had a first meeting luncheon that we walked over to after we'd settled into our cabin. I hated these meetings, it was always just another pissing contest between two packs who don't like each other.

I kept my eye on Bri as she wound her way through a set of kids close to her age. An up down look from one teenage boy brought a snarl to my throat. One major perk to shifter hearing? That little asshole heard me and made brief eye contact before staring at the ground. Damn right he better be embarrassed.

"Well well well, look at you being a dutiful big sister," Anthony's said from behind. I slowly turned to meet his smirk, trying to reign in my glare. His eyes traveled the length of my body, my skin crawling as he made his way slowly back up to my eyes. "I suppose your little sister may take after you in some ways, but I'm happy it was you that your dad promised."

"Funny thing that, last time I checked mates get to choose who they screw, not their dad's," I said, forcing a smile.

"Well, princess, it looks like your old man just has your best interests at heart. Any other female in this pack would be tripping over themselves to be my mate."

"By tripping over themselves, do you mean as they try to run away from you?" I asked, my polite tone slipping.

His eyes darkened, a dangerous glint taking over. He took a step forward, invading my space as easily as he would a bug he was about to squish.

"I'm only going to say this once, Hope. You are mine. I don't let anyone talk to me like that, so as much as I enjoy a little sass here and there, you need to learn how to keep that mouth shut," he said as he reached towards my lips.

"Unless you want me to bite a finger off," I spat through clenched teeth, any trace of a smile gone, "I would move."

His eyes widened and then narrowed. "Fine, I can take a hint," he said, chuckling. His hand dropped, but before I could feel any measure of relief, he grabbed my arm. Hard.

I could feel the rage boiling underneath my skin, my wolf's desire to rip his hand off of me almost overwhelming my control. My sister floated into view behind him, the worry in her eyes speaking volumes. She started to walk towards us, her jaw set. I shook my head slightly, mustering a smile. She paused and turned around quickly as Anthony looked between us.

"It's time to go sit, we are right over here," he said, his smile growing. He hooked an arm around my waist and started to guide me over to his table.

At least, he tried. My feet were glued to the floor, despite how much I knew I needed to play along.

"Hope, move your ass before I move it for you." He muttered out of the side of his mouth, somehow maintaining his smile while his tone turned to ice. "Unless this is what you really wanted this whole time? I don't mind announcing this right here and now." A growl snuck out as his hand grazed my ass.

Before I could unclench my jaw long enough to say anything, I felt someone come up behind us.

I'd know that scent anywhere.

Jensen.

"I would really suggest moving that hand before Hope rips it off." Jensen's voice was deadly calm, with just a hint of threat to it.

"That's one way to say hello, nephew. I suppose the customs in your pack are a little different in how mates treat each other, but Hope is more than fine." Dammit. Anthony's shit eating grin was back.

How the fuck was I supposed to marry this man and not slit

his throat in his sleep?

Jensen's glare shifted to me, his eyes unreadable. "Mate? I hadn't heard." He bit out.

"You haven't heard because it isn't official," I said in a rush. Why was he pissed? This had literally no impact on his pack, and he had made his disgust of me obvious over the years.

He paused for a minute, his eyes continuing to search mine.

Anthony looked between us, his eyes darkening.

"We were just discussing that, weren't we princess? The meeting tonight is the perfect place to announce it. Why wait?" He asked, pointedly staring at me and then shifting his eyes to where Bri was sitting. Message received asshole, it's me or her.

Forcing a smile that I am sure looked like I'd rather eat glass, I said, "We'll see."

Jensen looked between the two of us, his brow furrowed. "I guess we will. Well, I will see you both tonight at dinner." And he strode away. Not a backwards glance, how familiar was that.

It seemed like all I did at these godforsaken meetings was watch that man walk away.

# CHAPTER FOUR

*Jensen*

Mate.

Breathe in.

MATE.

Breathe out.

Unclenching my hands, I kept walking away. Even while everything in me screamed to turn around. To rip out Anthony's heart with my claws, watch his sneer fade into shock as his hands dropped from Hope's waist. From MY fucking waist.

This line of thinking was not helping.

"Jensen, you good?" Sam's questions startled me, bringing me out of my daydream.

"Yep. I'm great. You know, just trying to keep the peace."

"The peace? I thought you were getting ready to go to war. You look furious, why do you talk to her? You know it always ends badly."

"Woah. Always? We were friends for years, Sam." I bit out the last part, tasting shame at the past tense.

We should still be friends.

Hell, we should be more than that and I knew it.

"You certainly didn't look friendly talking to her." Sam's eyebrow quirked up as he looked past me at her. God, what I wouldn't give to be able to look at her whenever I wanted.

I'm not sure I would ever not be looking at her.

Breathe in.

And out.

"Anthony said they are going to be announcing their engagement tonight." I kept my voice as neutral as possible.

Sam's look of surprise confirmed what I already suspected. This WAS unexpected, and not just by me.

"Oh. Oh wow, okay. Isn't he like thirty years older than her? And, you know, a fucking asshole."

"Yep, to both of those things. I have no idea what's going on, but it's definitely not a mate connection."

"Do you want me to poke around? See what I can find out?"

This is why he was my beta. Poking around at this was purely curiosity for him, but he knew it meant something to me.

"I appreciate it, but I think I'll handle it. Do me a favor, see if you can distract Anthony in half an hour, I think I'll be able to get more out of her if he isn't around." My palms began to sweat. I knew where she'd be if she didn't have to talk to him. It was the one place I'd avoided since we were 19 - where I'd first realized exactly how much she meant to me and where I shut down any possible future we could have had.

"Alright, one annoying beta coming up," he said, rubbing his palms together with barely suppressed glee.

"Thanks Sam, I'm going to go set it up."

I walked outside the side door, feeling Anthony's eyes tracking me.

Thankfully, the rain had finally stopped. Why we always met during the rainiest time of the year was beyond me, I needed to bring that up at our meeting today.

The buildings around the conference hall were varied. Years ago, before I'd been born, the packs would stay in the cabins surrounding the hall, spending time with those they hadn't seen in a year. Something like that would lead to a wholesale slaughter at this point, ever since the Wildwood Pack tried to murder the Crescent River Pack's alphas' daughter and her future mate.

They also happened to be my parents.

The cabin closest to the lake was a favorite of mine. Of ours, really. My first trip here seemed like it was from another lifetime. My parents let my brother and I roam with our guards, but I shifted and ran away from mine while my brother pretended to be sick.

I'd run to the lake, hoping to go for a swim, and there she'd been, skipping rocks and looking like she'd rather be anywhere but there. I'd hidden next to the cabin, watching as she stomped around looking for another rock.

"I know you're there," She'd grumped out. "If we're going to have to be here, might as well come out."

I'd shifted, pulled on my pants, and walked around the corner. She'd been surprised, she told me later she thought I'd been her sister. We'd skipped rocks and talked about everything under the sun, and when the meeting went late, we went into the cabin and played some kind of card game. By the end of the trip, I knew that she was the oldest of two kids, that her mother had died five years ago, and that she was one of the most passionate people I'd ever met.

I also knew I loved her, even then.

My eyes swept over the cabin, it's sagging deck endearing in it's timelessness. We'd made a deal to meet there every year, and we did. For nine years, we swam, skipped rocks, and played games. I almost kissed her when we were seventeen. I almost told her I loved her at eighteen. At nineteen, I knew it would be our last week together.

I still remembered how she'd held back her tears. How I'd told her I wasn't coming back to the cabin next year, that we couldn't be friends anymore. She'd turned when I'd said friends, steely voiced "We were never friends."

I'd walked away, telling myself that I'd done what was right, what was *expected*. It didn't make me feel any better.

She'd gone back to the cabin every year, and I'd watched her glare and act as if we had never been anything other than enemies.

Shaking my head to clear the memories, I walked past the steps to the lake. The rain had finally let up, and the smooth stones were perfect for skipping.

My first toss made it 3 skips, the second 5. I was rooting around for the next rock when I heard her soft intake. I turned, trying to keep my face as neutral as possible, hoping she wouldn't walk away.

"What are you doing here, Jensen?" The sharpness in her tone was something I deserved, but damn if it didn't hurt.

"Well," I said, drawing it out, "Last I checked, you were not into men thirty years older than you. Mind telling me what the fuck that's about?"

# CHAPTER FIVE

*Hope*

"I'm sorry, what?" I looked around, expecting some kind of ambush. He hadn't been to the cabin in years, and now he wanted to talk about who I was "into"?

Nope. Don't like that.

His eyes drew to where Anthony's hands had been on my waist, lasering in on the exact spot as if he'd left a mark. I brushed at my shirt, wishing I could push away the feel of his eyes.

"I'm surprised, is all. Anthony has what, thirty years on you? And you looked less than thrilled about announcing your engagement. So what is it? I know Wildwood Pack is less than keen on honoring the females of their pack." He spit out, as if he would treat females any different. "Does that extend to forced marriages now?"

I walked down by the water, hoping some time would slow

my heart. He'd always been too good at reading me, and the last thing I needed was for him to piss of Anthony.

"It's not forced," I said, hoping my tone seemed neutral. Hopeful seemed like a stretch. "Some bonds are about more than love. Wildwood Pack is no less 'keen' on honor than Crescent River Pack, if our childhood was any indication."

He turned, and I swear I saw him flinch. Clenching his fists on an inhale, I felt relieved. All I had to do was piss him off a little more and I'd be free. Free to marry a revolting asshole to save my sister, sure, but at least I wouldn't feel the ache of carrying Jensen around.

"If that's the only reason you're here, why don't you head back. I'm fine with the way things are, and you brooding and invading my spot is a pain in th-"

His hand grazing mine made everything stop. My air. My thoughts. Whatever petty comment that was about to send him away. I looked down at my hand, frozen as he laced our fingers together.

"Hope. You used to be my best friend. We may not talk anymore, but I still know you. And I know this is not your choice. That he is not your choice. Please, let me help you." I swam in those deep brown eyes, the plea in them softening my irritation.

"It's not." I started then stopped, looking down at our hands again. Breathe, Hope, just breathe. You have held his hand a million times and then he left. It means nothing. It meant nothing to him then and it doesn't mean anything now.

"It's not that simple." Wait, what? Damn those eyes. He became, somehow, even more serious. He pulled me up the cabin steps, to our secret getaway. I hadn't been inside in years, couldn't bring myself to. The lake had been my spot before he'd come along, but the cabin?

The cabin had been ours.

"Sit," He said, pulling out the bench closest to the door. With a sigh, I sank down, hoping that the time to get the fire going would help me clear my head. And shut my freaking mouth. God. This man does not deserve your time, Hope. You have given more years than you have not to him, and he LEFT. He walked away and he avoided you. Hell, he's engaged.

Damn. Good pep talk, self.

"Aren't you engaged?" Not the most tactful way of asking, but I got it out.

God, I'd forgotten how he'd raise the one eyebrow when I said things he thought were ridiculous. It should be insulting, really. It should *not* be something I found sexy.

"Engaged? Definitely not." He sounded so final about it, it didn't leave much room for doubt.

I traced the swirls on the wooden table, making my way to the carved initials on the edge. God, we were so young.

*Hope & Jensen*

"It looks like we just carved that," he said, his voice right next to my ear.

"God! How did you get over here so quietly?" I yelped, jolting upright.

"Quietly? I was three feet away from you, Hope. You do know shifter hearing should be better than most, right? You might want to get that checked out." There was that teasing smile. I followed the crinkles by his eyes, all the way to the dimple in his right cheek. His cheekbones had sharpened since I'd last looked this closely at him; he looked like a man now. I felt my cheeks reddening, memories from years ago flooding the space.

"Yeah, well, you're being stealthy. Anyways, so you're not engaged. I'm almost engaged and it isn't forced. I think we are all caught up, anything else?" I asked breezily, hoping he would leave. *Mostly* hoping he would leave.

Okay, half-hoping.

I put my hands on the table, the indent of our initials a brand as I pushed against it to stand.

*Smack*

I looked down at the hand pinning mine in place over the initials.

"That meant something, once upon a time Hope. Please, hear me out."

Whether it was the physical contact or the please that did it, I sank back down to the bench, nodding as I went.

He watched me settle back in, a half-smile toying at his lips. That little quirk of his mouth was captivating, and it was all I could do to not sit and stare as he went from brooding asshole to, well, absolutely beautiful.

His smile grew as he watched, seeming to sense what I was thinking.

"You have to talk for me to 'hear you out,'" I snapped.

"Right," he chuckled. "Well, I'm not going to argue with you over whether I think this whole thing is bullshit. But I want you to know you don't have to do anything you don't want to do."

"Thank you for explaining free will to me, I had no idea. Is that all?"

"No, it isn't. On the completely off chance that this is not an engagement of your choosing, I can help you get out of it."

My mouth dried as I stared at him, trying to tamp down any belief in his offer. "Oh really? And how would you do that?"

"We could pretend to be fated mates and you could leave with me tomorrow," He said calmly, his face set.

I searched his face, looking for the joke that had to be there. There was only sincerity in his big brown eyes.

"You're kidding, right? That would start a war. Anthony would not stop until he had me, until he," I clamped my mouth shut, my pulse racing.

"Until he what Hope?"

Damn those eyes and their ability to wring the truth out of me.

"Nothing. It's nothing because that is not an option. I have family in my pack, Jensen. A life. Plus, do you know how many people want to be the alpha's mate? I'm lucky." The words felt like soot in my mouth, my stomach churning as I remembered recoiling at those exact words the day before.

"Lucky?" He bit out. "Lucky? Are you fucking kidding me Hope?"

He's angry?

He is fucking angry?

"Am I fucking kidding you? Are you fucking kidding me?" My voice was approaching a pitch that only dogs could hear, but I didn't care. He was angry with me for what? He may not have the entire picture, but how dare he.

I stood up, turning away from him as I gripped my hands together.

"Look Jensen, I don't know what the hell your endgame is here, but you have no idea what my life is like now. You made sure of that years ago, so whatever is pissing you off or making you think I'm some damsel in distress, tell it to kindly shut the fuck up and go back to your pack." I spat, moving towards the door.

He was against the door before I could open it.

"I'm sorry. I'm sorry Hope. You're right. I shouldn't have gotten mad. I did end things-"

"There was nothing to end." I muttered, hating how much pain was in my voice.

"You don't mean that," he said, taking both of my hands in his. I could feel his stare as I looked at our hands, my pale skin appearing translucent next to his.

"No," I whispered, "I don't." Steeling myself, I looked up into his eyes, trying to ignore for the hundredth time how they warmed me from the inside out.

"What happened between us was a long time ago. I'm getting married, Jensen. It's complicated, but my business is not yours anymore." I pulled away, straightening my shoulders as if for battle.

"What if I want it to be?" He murmured, tucking a stray hair behind my ear as he stepped closer.

Damn this man.

I stepped back, bumping into the table.

"Well, then I would say you should prepare to have an unfulfilled life." I quipped, hoping the flush I could feel coming on wouldn't be noticeable.

"Oh Hope, that's nothing new where you're concerned." He shot back, his eyes drinking me in.

As if he was actually interested in me.

"Mmhm. Okay. Well, this has been... Something. I need to get back before Brianna starts to worry." I moved past him, the knot in my stomach loosening when he didn't move to stop me.

"I don't care if it starts a war, Hope. I don't know what he has on you, but I can keep you safe. I can keep Brianna safe. And if I am even a little right about this not being your choice, please know you have another option."

I turned back, surprised by how close he had gotten. He leaned down, the scent of pine and something delicious enveloping me as he pressed a kiss to my forehead. "Please. Just think about."

I nodded, not trusting my voice to make it past the lump in my throat. Pulling the door open, I all but ran from the cabin, hoping the fresh air would ease the pounding of my heart.

# CHAPTER SIX

## *Jensen*

I leaned against the door frame, replaying what had just happened.

"Just think about it."

I gripped the frame tighter as I thought of the fear I'd seen flash across her face. She'd reigned it in, like she always did, but it had been there in the pinch of her nose, her quick breaths, her clenched jaw. I'd barely stopped myself from wrapping her in my arms and promising to end whoever the fuck was causing her that tension.

Pretty sure their name started with an A.

Even more sure that I wanted to murder him.

I stood up and pulled out my phone to see Sam calling.

"What's up?" I asked, noticing a crack on the door frame. I did not realize how tight I had been holding it.

"The eagle has flown, I repeat, the eagle has flown." He half whispered, his tone urgent.

"Uh, what are you talking about?"

He chuckled. "Anthony has officially left the pavilion. I think he was done discussing how the wildlife has been doing this season."

"That's how you distracted him?"

"Hey, it worked. I told him that we had heard his pack had taken down some big bucks and I wanted to know how they were so skilled at it. Stroke the ego a little and the man won't shut up."

I laughed, shaking my head as I headed out of the cabin. A quick scan told me Hope had disappeared. Which was good, technically. The last thing we needed was for Anthony to see us exiting the same cabin.

Then again, that would be one way to start a fight.

"What are you smirking about?" Sam's voice startled me as he came walking up. "Did you just jump?" He asked, his smile growing as he put his hand to my forehead. "You feeling okay?"

"I'm fine," I said, shoving his hand away. "I was just thinking, you surprised me."

His smile grew as he stared at me and shifted his gaze to the cabin. "Anything you need to tell me?"

"Nothing definite yet. I'll let you know."

"Okay," He drawled. "Do I want to know why you are so on edge?"

"Nope." I said, drawing my hand over my eyes. "I need to go for a run, can you keep an eye on everything while I'm out?"

"Sure, do you want someone to go with? I can go find Leo."

"No. I need to be alone," I said, scanning the forest by the cabin. "I won't be gone long."

"Okay, I'll see you soon." He said, turning back to the pavilion.

I strode towards the woods, the full moon pulling at my wolf. When I was younger, I could only go out for a run during the full moon if one of my parents was with me. Every wolf responds to the moon differently, but alpha wolves are strongest then, and mine never wanted to shift back to human.

I left my clothes next to the giant weeping willow and allowed my wolf to take over. He had been restless all day.

Between the inevitable power struggle when more than one alpha was present and then everything with Hope, we both needed a run.

We ran down to the lake, the cool water soothing our thirst. I let my wolf take over, running as fast as he could through the trees. It was a relief to focus solely on the woods, the peace found in the darkness and solitude.

The sound of hushed voices snapped me back to attention. Shifter hearing was enhanced when in your human form, but wolf hearing was on another level.

I crept forward towards the sound, staying far enough away that even a shifter would be unable to hear. Staying low to the ground, we came up to a clearing with Anthony and the Wildwood Pack witch.

Thankfully there was no wind to carry my scent, or I wouldn't have been able to get close enough.

"What the fuck do you mean you can't do it?" Anthony growled, unsheathing his claws.

The witch clenched her jaw, lifting her head up as she spoke. "You can't force a mating. There is no spell I know of that can make someone your mate."

"Then what the fuck are you good for?" He roared, any pretense of control slipping as his eyes began to glow.

"I can't make her mate with you, Anthony. But there are other spells, other means of control I can use to keep her close to you." She stuttered, stumbling away from him as he stalked closer.

Anthony stopped in his tracks, a smirk on his face. "Well, why didn't you start with that. What do you need?"

"Give me until tomorrow afternoon. Once you announce your

engagement, we can perform a ceremony. You can tell her it's customary for mating to the alpha, to mix your blood at the announcement. Once she willingly does so, she won't be able to leave your pack territory." The witch's words tumbled out, her eyes focused on the ground.

"That's more fucking like it Ellie. Between this and the prophecy, I guess I'm glad I saved you all those years ago."

I crept away from the clearing, my thoughts reeling. He was going to bind her to his territory.

My wolf wanted to turn around and rip him apart. It took everything in me to quietly jog back to the willow. I shifted back, stiffly putting my clothes back on.

I had to get Hope and her sister out of here. No voluntary marriage required a spell forcing them to stay on your territory, no matter what she claimed she was okay with.

How the hell was I supposed to convince her when she wouldn't even admit this was against her will?

# CHAPTER SEVEN

## *Hope*

"Just think about it."

Those four words had been playing on repeat for the past several hours, and it was safe to say sleep was not going to come easily tonight. I knew that I could count on him to keep Brianna and I safe, but to leave our pack? Our home? What's happening with Anthony is awful, of course, but it's not like I had faith that being engaged to Jensen would be much better.

It was no good, I needed to walk. Or even better, run.

I slipped out from under my blankets, silently congratulating myself on avoiding the creaky floorboard next to my bed.

"Hope? Are you going somewhere?"

Apparently not that quietly.

"I'm sorry Bri, I didn't mean to wake you up. I was just going to go for a run, get some insomnia out."

"Still thinking about Jensen's offer?" She asked, rolling towards me with a knowing smile. She had an uncanny ability to read my mind, even when I didn't want to talk about it.

"Eh. Only a little. I'm not even sure he meant it, and even if he did, could we really leave? They're our pack, our home."

"Home doesn't look like that, Hope. And a real pack sure as hell doesn't act like ours." The bitterness there surprised me. I knew Bri had been exposed to more than I wanted her to; there was only so much you can do in a small house with a loud drunk for a father, but I thought she had at least some positive connections in the pack.

"Sure as hell doesn't, huh? Here I thought you would be more against this idea than I am," I said, fidgeting with my nails. I hadn't realized how much I was counting on her resisting the move.

"Against it? Seriously? This is our chance to get out. And, if that was the only reason, that would be enough. But the way you two have always looked at each other?" She questioned, a smirk hovering in the moonlight. "Well that will make for some *interesting* dynamics in our family. I can't wait to see what you two are like once you're married."

Married. Oh God. that's what people do when they get engaged. It ends in marriage, how had I not put those two together.

"Okay, he did not offer marriage. He said we could pretend to be engaged."

Bri shook her head, still smirking.

"Did he say it would end without getting married?"

"He didn't have to! I am the last person he would want to marry! And twice over for me!" I pulled on my coat and shot her a look. "I wanted to go for a run to help calm down about this, not freak out more."

"Well, sorry for not helping you avoid your problems," she chuckled and her eyes became more serious. "Can we also address that your 'problem' is that a gorgeous alpha wants to pretend to be your mate and whisk you away from a life of abuse?"

I snorted at her description. "It's not that simple, and you know it."

"It isn't, but the fact that he's willing to do this is huge. I know this needs to be your decision, and I will support you either way, but I am all for going. I would love to see what a functional pack looks like," she smiled at me, curling her hair around one finger. "Besides, there are some gorgeous boys in that pack."

I laughed at that, my concern over her thoughts melting away and leaving me relieved. And more confused.

"Okay, I really need some fresh air. I'll be back soon, try to get some sleep."

I stepped outside, reveling in how warm it still was. My thoughts drifted to my mom as I walked over to the lake. I didn't remember much about coming here with her, but I did remember how much she had loved the water.

The pack meetings were my favorite back then. Dad was so busy following Anthony around that it was just the two of us. We didn't have to worry about what would set him off or stay quiet and out of the way. We could just be. Our last summer here was when Bri was a baby.

I remembered how hard she'd laughed when Bri tried to eat a fistful of sand, her mouth shaking as she tried to fit her entire fist in her mouth. The sun had gleamed against Mom's curls, the red almost blinding in the glare. My heart ached at the memory and I couldn't help but wonder if this is how she felt when she was about to get married. Alone and helpless.

What would she say if she was still alive? Would she still be with my dad?

Could we have escaped before I was forced into marrying Anthony?

The sound of footsteps yanked me back to the present. I wiped the corner of my eye, hoping whoever it was didn't notice I had been crying.

"Hope?" The voice was soft and familiar.

"Leo," I said, smiling and reaching out to give him a hug. "You look more like your brother every year. How are you?"

He chuckled, his eyes crinkling at the edges. "I was good until you said I look like Jensen. Are you trying to hurt my feelings?" He joked, putting his hand to his chest. I laughed at his exaggerated outrage.

"I apologize, I promise to never compare you to him," I said solemnly, "at least, not until next year."

"Ha ha, very funny. What are you doing out here by yourself?" He asked while he reached down for a rock. I watched as he tried to skip it, smirking as it only made three jumps before sinking.

"Well, I definitely didn't come out to watch that," I said, my voice light. How much did he know about what his brother had asked me? Would he support Jensen or would he see the danger and do what was best for his pack?

Leo had always wanted to tag along with Jensen and I when we were kids, and we would let him sometimes, but we had become better friends over the last six years. Even with that history, I didn't think he would be on board with starting a war.

No one could be worth that.

"Hope?" He asked, staring at me.

"Yes?" I asked, hoping he wouldn't bring it up. I couldn't handle another Valenzuela brother's pity.

"I asked if you were really engaged? Jensen has been an ass since you two spoke earlier and Sam said you and Anthony were together?"

Dammit.

"An ass huh? Is that really that outside of the norm for Jensen?" I said, the bitterness seeping in and making the joke fall flat.

"I know, I know," he said, raising his hands. "We don't talk about him, and I get it. You two love each other but you're not together, it's tragic, yada yada."

"Wait, what?" I sputtered, my eyes widening as his smile grew.

"Sorry, broke another rule. Since we are not speaking of the alpha-who-must-not-be-named, can we please discuss why you are marrying my old, demon of an uncle?"

I shook my head, trying to clear my thoughts. Love each other? I'm pretty sure any love we felt was murdered, chopped into tiny pieces, cremated, and the ashes thrown over a cliff when he ended our friendship.

Or whatever we'd been.

"I'm not marrying him," I said, sighing. "At least, not yet. We haven't announced the mating ceremony but I think we will before the meeting is over."

"You can't be serious?" He asked, raising his voice. "Hope, you can't do that. There's a reason we never talk to him and he's our *family*. We don't get to choose who our blood is, but you get to choose your mate," he said, his words an uncomfortable echo.

"I don't want to talk about it, Leo. It's happening," I said, resigned. "Can we just go back to skipping rocks. Why don't you tell me about your girlfriend?" I asked hopefully, grabbing another rock and sending it skipping across the lake. "Or we could just have a rock skipping competition? That was at least seven skips."

He stared at me, obviously debating whether he should keep talking about Anthony.

"Please, Leo," I said softly. "I can't do more of this today." I wasn't sure what I even meant. More talk about Anthony? More hating how I feel about Jensen? It felt like I had been hit by an emotional semi truck and I just wanted to have a break.

He nodded, his eyes softening. "Okay. First one to fifteen skips wins?"

"Deal."

# CHAPTER EIGHT

## *Jensen*

I peered through the window, watching as Hope stepped out of her cabin. I'd been hoping she would come out so I could check in with her, but it had been quiet. She walked over to the shore, staring across the lake's surface.

I noticed someone ambling up, irritation surfacing until I realized who it was. Leo. He always made it a point to see her at the meetings. I knew it was good for her to have someone looking out for her, and I wasn't going to be angry at him for seeing her.

Or for hugging her. I scowled at their embrace. Why did he take so long to let go? What the fuck was he up to? I growled quietly, jealousy burning my gut.

"Earth to Jensen?" Sam asked, his voice sounding from right behind me.

I jumped around, embarrassed that he had caught me

watching her.

"Sorry, what was that?" I asked, trying to sound nonchalant. Sam rolled his eyes, his grin growing as he looked past me to the window.

"I asked what the plan was for tomorrow, but I'm assuming you're a little more focused on what Hope is doing?" His grin widened as I clenched my jaw and walked away from the window.

"I don't have a plan for tomorrow yet," I said, gripping the back of my neck. "There have been some new developments since earlier."

"New as in Hope is pregnant with your child and we are whisking her away?"

My wolf whined at the description as a pulse of longing panged through me.

"Very funny. Yes, it's a miraculous conception considering I haven't seen her in months. She's having a wolf Jesus." I said snarkily, ignoring Sam's laugh.

"The new development is that Anthony is, somehow, an even worse asshole than we thought. He and his witch are planning to use a blood spell to keep Hope trapped on his pack lands once they return home."

"The fuck?" He said, eyes widening. "Did you know that was possible?"

"No," I bit out. "It's not like Elena practices that kind of magic. Even if someone could, I can't imagine an alpha being okay with that."

"Wow. Okay, what do you want me to do?" He asked, looking past me again to Hope, concern clear on his face.

"Nothing yet. I need to talk with Hope and see if I can get her to agree to come with us. The last thing she needs is to feel like she is going from one forced relationship to another." I turned back to the window, wishing she was here.

"And if she doesn't agree?" Sam looked past me, his eyes scanning the other cabins.

"Then I'll tell her about the spell. If she still decides to go, after all of that and knowing we will keep her and Bri safe, then that's her choice." My wolf was thrashing around and whining at the thought.

"You would let her go?" He asked, his voice heavy with shock. I turned to him, grimacing.

"There is no 'letting' her. I'm not in charge of her, and whatever our relationship looks like in the future, I will not be another person in her life who takes away her choices." As horrible as letting her stay was, I meant it.

"I need to call Elena and go over what I heard today. I'll see you in the morning."

"Okay, call if you need anything else. I'll just prepare for a few different scenarios." He said, a hint of a smile on his face as he left. "Want me to tell Leo to get away from her?" He called from the porch, chuckling to himself as the door shut.

"Hilarious." I said loudly enough that he could hear me. I took a deep breath, knowing I would need to stay calm for this next conversation. I pulled my phone out and saw that Elena was calling. Of course she beat me to it. I smiled, a measure of reassurance washing over me as I answered.

"Hi big bro. Why is my wolf freaking out?" My smile grew at her tone.

"Oh no reason, you know, just your average All Pack meeting," I said, wondering how much she already knew.

"Really? Because I can't seem to stop thinking of Hope today. Which hasn't happened in six years. I keep seeing the two of you together. What is going on over there?"

"The two of us together? As in fighting or talking?" I asked, hoping she knew what would happen tomorrow.

"Talking, being in the same room, down by the lake. Either way, there seemed to be some heavy emotions. I also saw Anthony looking like he was ready to rip someone's head off. Please tell me you're safe." Her concern barely registered as my thoughts raced.

An angry Anthony hopefully meant he didn't get his way. That she leaves with us. I let out a sigh, the knot in my chest easing.

"Did you just sigh? None of those things sounded like a good thing to me."

"It's hard to explain, but I need to talk to you about something else. I have a question about blood spells."

"Blood spells? Okay, what the hell Jensen. Do I need to drive down there?" I could hear her moving around, the sound of drawers opening.

"No, it's not that urgent. I just need to know if they work."

"That's a complicated question. And not one I'm great with, blood magic is very rarely allowed in our pack, you know that."

"What about a spell that binds someone to a pack's territory? Is that possible?"

"Honestly, I'm not sure. I think it would be, but the level of power needed to sustain a spell like that would be... Monumental. The blood binding the person would need to be powerful as well. Alpha level."

"Would they need to be on the pack lands to do it?"

"Not necessarily. But they sure as hell would need to haul ass back or the person could die."

My gut dropped. Fucking Anthony. How he and my dad came from the same parents was impossible to even comprehend.

"Is there any way to stop it from happening?" I asked, trying to stay calm. My wolf was not helping, I could feel him stretching at my skin, trying to force the shift.

"Once it's happened? Not that I know of, but the blood has to be given willingly."

I closed my eyes as relief flooded through me. "Thank you sis. Seriously. I'll explain everything when I get home," I promised, knowing she would wait until I was back to interrogate me, and not a minute longer.

"I'll hold you to it," she said, her tone softening, "Be careful and I better see you here in two days."

"You will. Love you," I said and ended the call.

I just had to stop Hope from giving her blood. And convince her to come home with me.

I grimaced. Not a big deal at all.

# CHAPTER NINE

## *Hope*

"Hope? Is that you?" My jaw clenched at the fake syrup dripping off of every word. Lily. I turned, managing what I hoped was a passable grin.

Hell, I'd settle for anything warmer than a glare.

"It is! Oh my goodness, I had no idea you were coming," she said, leaning in to give me a brief, overly perfumed squeeze. "Have you seen Jensen? He ran off this morning before I could talk to him."

Ran off?

This **morning**?!

Son of a fucking bitch.

"I haven't seen him." I tried, really, I *tried* to keep my voice neutral, but something must have given me away.

Lily watched me, a smirk playing at the edges of her mouth. "Oh, well I thought maybe you had. You two used to be so... Close. Well, if you see him before I do, please tell him I'm looking for him."

The hell I would.

Giving a short nod, I spun on my heels and made my way to the breakfast buffet. So much for not being with anyone. Why the hell would I agree to a fake engagement to someone if he has someone else on the side?

Shoving a mini muffin into my mouth to stop any further growls from slipping out, I started loading up a plate with every carb I could find. Who said you couldn't eat your feelings?

"Hope?"

Oh no. Not now. I chewed faster, swallowing and half choking myself as I turned to Jensen.

"Hey," I croaked, "Lily is looking for you. It seemed pretty important, you should probably go find her."

"It's fine, it's probably just about the agenda for today."

"Oh, is that what they call it in Crescent River?" I muttered, turning to grab another muffin.

"What?"

"Nothing. It's nothing. I need to go find Bri."

"She's sitting over there with Leo, she'll be fine for a minute." He stepped closer, lowering his voice to a whisper, "Can we go talk outside?"

I should feel pissed. Or, at the bare minimum, betrayed. Did I? No, my stupid heart was working overtime.

"Look Jensen, I'm starving, your favorite pack member wants you because you slipped out this morning before she could talk to you. Could you please just let me eat in peace." I turned on my heel and started towards Bri's table, cheeks on fire. Two steps, that's as far as I made it, before he grabbed my arm.

"I don't know what Lily said," My eyes traveled down to the hand on my arm, anger and something else, something I did *not* want to think about, warring at it's touch. "I have never in my life thought of her as my favorite anything, and I saw her for the first time this morning at our pack meeting."

Damn those dark eyes and their sincerity. I closed my eyes, hoping that being unable to see them would at least give me space to think.

"Okay. Well, it doesn't matter either way, you don't owe me anything."

And wasn't that the truth? It shouldn't sting like it did. This was just an opportunity to leave, one I hadn't even made up my mind about yet.

Sparks flew over my skin as his hand moved to mine, lacing

our fingers together. I couldn't stop looking at our entwined hands if my life depended on it. And if Anthony came in and saw us? It very well could depend on it.

"Please Hope. Can we go talk?" He asked gently, slowly walking towards exit. "I don't want to do this here."

I nodded and went with him, trying to regain some semblance of control. He walked faster over to his cabin, his long strides eating up the sidewalk. I wasn't short, by any means, but I felt like a toddler trying to keep up with him.

He brought us over to the porch swing at his cabin; it faced the lake so no one would see us unless they came around the corner first.

"Why do you get a swing?" I asked, pulling my hand from his and sitting down. "I don't think any of the other cabins have these?"

"They don't," he said with a soft smile. "My parents brought it with us one year when Elena was a baby. She was constantly fussing, and the only things that helped her go to sleep were car rides or rocking." He sat down next to me and looked out at the lake.

"Things were easier then," he laughed quietly. "I'm sure every adult feels that way. We don't know how lucky we are until it's time to be responsible."

I turned away, my eyes filling with tears. Not every adult. I could feel his eyes on me, burning a hole in the back of my head.

"What is it?" he probed gently, wrapping his arm around me. The simple gesture was enough for the tears to well over. I swiped at them angrily, shooting to my feet.

"Why do you care?" I asked, suddenly furious. "Why do you suddenly care about anything to do with me? We," I motioned between us, "have not cared about each other in a long damn time."

His shock turned to irritation as he pointed a finger at me. "I never once stopped caring about you, Hope. Don't assume you know how I've felt."

"Are you kidding me? It's not much of an assumption," I yelled, throwing my arms wide, "We spoke more yesterday than we have in six years!"

Jensen opened his mouth and then took a deep breath. "You're right," he said softly, "I have done a shit job at showing how much you mean to me."

He stood up and reached for my hand, pausing to see if I would pull away. When I didn't, he wrapped my hand in both of his and looked at me with eyes full of concern. "I want to make it right, Hope. Please let me."

I looked out at the lake, fighting down the panic I felt. Leaving with him made sense, logically. And I wanted desperately to keep Bri safe.

"Okay," I said, lifting my eyes to his. "I'll do it."

The smile he gave me was so wide and full of joy that I almost forgot what I needed to talk about.

"I'll do it on one condition," I continued. "We can pretend to be fake mates, we can even be friends again, but we will never be real mates."

# CHAPTER TEN

## *Jensen*

I stared at her, trying to keep my face neutral. The relief punching through me almost took my feet out from under me.

"If that's what you want, then that's what we'll do," I said evenly. "Just out of curiosity, are you opposed to all mates or just me?"

She made a face at me, the tension lifting. "All mates. I know what fate looked like for my mom and honestly, it seems like a shit deal."

"Why is that?" I asked, trying to remember anything about her mom. I'd been six when she would have died, but I only found out that when Hope and I started spending time together. "All I know about your dad is that he promised you to that asshole Anthony. And he seems to be drunk most of the time. I know losing your mate can be... unimaginable, but that's no excuse to treat your daughter like property."

"Yeah, well, I wish that he had changed because of my mom's death. If anything..." She turned towards the lake again, her eyes wistful.

"If anything?" I probed, wondering just how much damage he had done.

"It's nothing. He has always been too much. I don't even think it's being drunk that makes it worse. I honestly think that he feels like he is owed everything. His daughters' perfect obedience, control over us and everyone, and the right to force anyone who doesn't listen." Her fists clenched on the last part.

"Hold on." My wolf was thrashing around, trying to shift. It wanted to go rip him apart.

He wasn't the only one.

"When you say the right to "force anyone," what exactly are you talking about?"

"Let's just say that rapid healing feels less like a perk when someone knows they can be less careful where they punch. Who cares if it won't be noticeable tomorrow?" she said, the bitterness in her voice making my stomach feel hollow.

"He hit you?" He was a dead man. A motherfucking dead man.

"Not just me, all of us. I did my best to shield Bri, but I know she saw more than any kid should ever have to see."

"She wasn't the only kid in that house, Hope. What would your mom do?"

"Why do people always ask that?" She asked, shooting me a glare. "Like it's some moral failing of hers if, while she was passed out from a beating, my dad decided he wanted another person to beat the shit out of." I could tell I'd touched a nerve, the aura of her wolf was pressing on mine and she was not happy.

"I didn't mean it like that, I just mean..." What did I mean? "I guess part of me did, and you're right. I'm sure she did the absolute best she could to keep you safe. It's not like she was the one hurting you. I'm sorry."

"Thank you. Anyways, that's why I think fated mates are bullshit."

"Wait... Are those the only fated mates you have ever known? Your parents?" There was no way my teeth wouldn't crack under the grinding I was doing.

"I mean, other people claim they know of other couples, but yes. They were the only ones I actually knew and that was one too many." Her eyes had drifted down, and I watched as tears seemed to gather in the corners. She gave her head a little shake, trying to keep it together.

"I know you can love your family, and I know my mom loved us with everything she had. But romantic love? It's just another way to con someone, you know?"

"In what way?"

"Well, if someone is your fated mate, you don't leave them because if it's fate, they should treat you right. But if they don't, is it you who's the problem or fate?"

"Fate isn't an excuse to abuse your mate."

"Yeah, well, it sure made it easier for him to beat the shit out of all of us."

Fuck. I could feel my vision turning red. Son of a bitch. I took a few deep breaths as I closed my eyes and turned towards the cabin.

She stepped towards me, "Jensen? Are you okay?"

"Yep." Not even fucking close. "I'm so sorry you went through that. I'm sorry he ever did that to any of you. None of you deserved that." But he sure as hell did.

Breathe in.

And out.

"Thank you. Anyways, if you want to do this, it'll stay fake. I'm not worried about me having a problem with that, but if it is going to be for you, then let me know and I'll take my chances with Anthony."

"Well, even though I disagree about love, I promise to keep this fake."

My wolf growled.

Loudly.

"I need to work out some details about when we will leave as a pack, what do you want to do about your pack?"

"I don't know yet. I can't decide if things would go smoother if we announced it as we left or if it was in private."

I smiled as I imagined Anthony's face when we announce it. His reaction alone would make my day.

"I think that announcing it in public would stop him from trying to attack anyone, so that's probably our best bet."

"Alright, well let me know when we are leaving and I'll meet you at the pavilion."

"Okay, I'll text you."

By the time my restless feet brought me to Sam's cabin, my wolf was stretching at my skin, begging to let off some steam. On Hope's fucking sperm donor.

"Uh, Jensen? Why can I feel how pissed off your wolf is?" He asked, moving slowly toward me as if he was afraid I would explode.

"Because I'm fucking furious. I want to murder her Dad. Fucking END him."

"Whose Dad? Hope's?"

"What other fucking Dad, Sam? The fucking asshole beat them. He claimed that he and her mom were fated mates, which I don't believe for a fucking second, and then he routinely beat the ever loving shit out of them. And I think there was more that she wasn't saying, but I'm not going to pry." I sucked in a breath. "I'm just going to kill the fucking bastard."

"Oh okay, kill him. No big deal right? Just the beta of our rival pack. Good, solid plan."

"Okay, tone down the sarcasm. I didn't say I was going to do it today. But I will be the one to end him. I want him to feel just how fucked he was the second he touched them."

"Who's fucked?" Leo asked, bounding up the the cabin steps.

"Hope's Dad," I snapped, glaring at him.

"Whoa," he said, holding up his hands and raising a brow. "I'm not her dad, cool it."

"Why were you holding her last night?" I growled, shooting Sam a look when he laughed.

"Holding her?" He asked, smiling. "Do you mean when I hugged her? For like two seconds?"

"Sure looked like longer. Since when did you two hug?"

"Since forever. Just because you decided to freeze her out, doesn't mean I have to," He said, jutting out his chin. "You don't get to have her on hold, Jensen. She isn't yours."

I started to walk towards him with a snarl when Sam stepped between us.

"Knock it off," he said, glaring at both of us. "Leo, stop making it sound like you have a thing for Hope. We both know that's bullshit." He turned to me, "Jensen. Get your shit together. You can't murder her dad and get her away from Anthony. Pick one and then get ready, because either one of those means war."

I looked at my feet for a second as my rage cooled. I would never pick revenge over saving her.

"You're right," said Leo, "We're just friends, Jensen. That's all we've ever been, she's like a sister to me."

I looked up, relieved to see the sincerity in his eyes.

"I'm sorry man. I just want to keep her safe," I took a deep breath and continued. "She's coming back with us, she's my fated mate." My stomach twisted at the lie, but I knew the less people who knew, the safer she would be.

"For real?" He asked as his face lit up. "That's amazing! Congratulations!" He pulled me in for a hug, laughing. Any concerns I had about him having feelings for her evaporated at his sincere excitement.

"Mom and Dad are going to go nuts!" My stomach dropped at the mention of my parents. They were sickeningly in love and why I had so much faith in fated mates.

It's also why they'd be a hell of a lot harder to convince.

# CHAPTER ELEVEN

## *Hope*

The walk back to my cabin had been a torturous one. I didn't generally talk about my mom, let alone share what it was like growing up in that house.

I eased my way into the cabin, torn between wanting to talk to Bri and wanting to pack first and explain at the last possible second before we left. She would be thrilled and probably a little too triumphant when she found out that she had been right. Pulling our bags out from under our beds, I grabbed our dirty clothes and started to separate them.

"Hope?" Bri called as she walked in. She closed the door softly, the question in her eyes loud enough for me to hear. Looks like there wouldn't be any wait time.

"We're going with Jensen," I said begrudgingly, not even bothering to hide my irritation.

"Yeah we are!" She said, pumping her fist. "Why do you look less than excited? We're getting out, Hope. Finally."

I paused, looking around for any clothes I had missed and trying to calm my racing heart. "It's not going to be as easy as just walking out. They are going to try to stop us, and it won't stop once we're gone. Plus, how the hell am I supposed to act? I haven't.. I've never... I have no idea how to be fake fated mates!" I shouted the last little bit, the panic I had been trying to keep at bay spilling out. Turning towards the window, I traced the outlines of the panes, my breaths coming in short and fast.

I felt Bri's arms wrap around me, her head resting on my back. "Everything will be okay. I know this is sudden, and you have the weight of everyone's expectations as well as our safety pulling you down. You don't have to carry that alone."

I turned, wrapping her in a hug. "How is it you know exactly the right thing to say?"

She shrugged as she pulled away. "It's a gift. Now, what else still needs packed?"

"I haven't grabbed anything out of the bathroom, just the clothes in here." I knelt down, looking under our beds as my thoughts began to race again.

How were we supposed to tell everyone and leave intact?

"Have you two decided how you'll tell Anthony?" She asked, reading my thoughts.

I shook my head. "Nope. I don't even know if we will. It's

tempting to just take off in the middle of the night, but I know he'll come after us sooner if we do that."

"Do you think Dad will try to stop you?" She asked, the worry in her voice easing mine. We couldn't both fall apart.

"Even if he does, we will be okay," I said firmly. "He can try all he wants, but we're both getting out." I gave her a small smile, hoping she couldn't hear how badly I wanted to believe my own words.

"You're right. We're getting out!" She reached over and gave me another hug. "I know you're worried about a million things, but can we just stop for a minute and imagine how much better things are going to be?"

"I know," I said, her enthusiasm making me laugh. "I can't believe we won't ever have to go back to that house." My eyes began to water as I thought of our mom. "Do you think she would be disappointed in us?" I asked, hating that I was asking her for comfort.

"Not for even a second," she said. "I may not remember her, but I know she didn't want this for us. No real parent would."

"I love that," I chuckled. "Can we call Dad a fake parent from here on out?"

She laughed at that and went back to packing. We gathered everything except what we needed for the next day and settled into our beds.

"Do you think we'll come back here again?" Bri's voice cut

through the darkness long after I'd assumed she was asleep.

"I do," I murmured, "It may be a long time, but we'll make it back here."

I laid in bed for a long time thinking about the next day. Would anyone try to stop us? How could I make sure Bri stayed safe? Would Jensen still want to do this?

I finally drifted off into a restless sleep. My alarm went off after what felt like only a few minutes of sleep, but I was able to wake up pretty quickly when I remembered what we were doing.

A knock on the door jolted Bri and I both out of our beds.

"Who is it?" she whispered, trying to peer through my window.

"I don't know," I said quietly, "But it's way too early for someone to just stop by."

"What if this someone brings breakfast?" Jensen called through the door.

Bri laughed and grabbed her sweatshirt before opening the door.

"Hey future brother-in-law," she said slyly, laughing at his panicked expression.

"Uh, hey?" He said, looking at me.

"It's okay, she knows about the whole thing," I said, sparing him further worry.

"Whew, okay good. I didn't know if I needed to act like we were really together, I was worried you'd slap me if I tried to kiss you."

Oh no. We'd have to.. We'd have to kiss. I stood frozen, my brain trying to catch up and listen to Jensen and Bri's conversation. I watched him hand her the breakfast, my eyes glued to his lips. Were they as soft as I always thought they'd be?

He turned to me, saying something that went right over my head.

"Sorry, what?" I asked, blinking rapidly. Not the time Hope, this is not the time.

His smile widened as he stared at me, his eyes taking on a knowing glint.

"I was just saying that we need to talk about how we are going to make it out of here."

My stomach dropped as the reality of what we were trying to do set in. I grabbed a muffin off of the plate he'd handed Bri and took a bite, barely tasting it.

"What'd you have in mind?"

"Well, we don't need to stay until the last meeting tomorrow, so I'm leaning towards just getting it over with. Everyone is at the pavilion for breakfast, including Anthony and your dad. We could go in, announce it while most of my pack is around us, and leave as a group." He stated it all so calmly, his eyes confident.

"Okay, and what happens if an all out brawl starts?" I ask, doubting that it could really be that easy. Jensen's eyes softened as he reached for my hand.

"We know they won't take this well. We already know that."

"That is not reassuring," I said, yanking my hand away.

"I wasn't done," he said, chuckling. "I doubt my uncle will try anything here, not when he's outnumbered. We just need to get back to Crescent River and we'll have triple the security we do here."

I nodded, resisting the urge to pace.

"Okay, then let's get this over with," he said, his eyes searching mine for a minute. "Can you give us a minute, Brianna?"

"Sure," she said with a sly smile. "I'll put our stuff on the porch." We stared at each other while she took her time grabbing the bags, her smile widening when I shot her a look. "Okay, okay, I'm going."

I shook my head and released the breath I was holding when she finally left.

"Are you sure you want to do this?" Jensen asked, his

expression serious. I couldn't tell if he was asking because he wanted to make sure I knew I had a choice or because he wanted me to change my mind.

"Are you asking because you don't want me to?" I asked, the worry slipping out before I could stop it. His eyes widened and he took a step towards me to grab both of my hands.

"Not at all. You're in an impossible situation and I want to make sure that you have as much control over it as possible," he said, squeezing my hands. The easy way he touched me after all these years of not even speaking was unsettling, to say the least. I remembered this version of him, the one who was protective and sought any excuse to hold my hand, hug me, or press a kiss to my forehead.

I used to think that if he would just act that way again, it would make up for all the time we'd lost.

It didn't; it just made me that much more aware of all I'd been missing. Which really made it difficult to continue hating him.

"Why do you say shit like that?" I muttered, stepping away to look out the window. "Never mind, don't answer that. Let's just get this over with."

"That's one way to talk about our engagement," he said wryly. "Lead the way."

# CHAPTER TWELVE

## *Jensen*

I followed Hope out of her cabin, scanning the area surrounding it for signs of anyone. I assumed Anthony would have someone from their pack watching her, but there hadn't been anyone this morning. Cocky bastard; he knew he had her trapped. Hell, he was probably planning on announcing their engagement this morning, too.

I laughed softly, imagining his face when he realized that not only is she leaving his pack and him, she's leaving it to be with me. Hope turned, her eyes questioning.

"It's nothing," I said. We found Brianna waiting outside of the pavilion, shifting between her feet nervously. Sam came out just as we walked up to the entrance, his eyes searching mine. I gave him a nod and he sighed in relief and turned to Hope.

"I'll go pack everything, where are your bags?" He asked. Hope pointed wordlessly by Brianna's feet and started fidgeting with the zipper on her coat.

We needed to get this over with before someone noticed how anxious she was.

"Okay Brianna, my pack is sitting up front. Leo should have a seat saved for you. We'll go in together so no one has the chance to notice anything is off before I make the announcement." I tried to put them at ease as much as I could, but I could see how little of an impact it had.

I couldn't help but admire how they both nodded with their jaws clenched and raised their chins, preparing for battle.

I reached over and squeezed Hope's hand one last time before I walked in with them trailing me. Brianna went immediately to sit by Leo while Hope stood slightly behind me.

Anthony was standing towards the back by the buffet, Hope's dad speaking quietly to him. Whatever Jason was saying, Anthony already looked angry. I sent Hope one last smile, took a deep breath, and stepped a little closer to the middle of the room.

"Hello everyone, I would like to make an announcement," I yelled, clapping my hands together. Conversations across the room died out as everyone turned to me. Anthony looked turned towards me and his eyes immediately noticed Hope behind me. He snarled as he started to slowly make his way to the front, edging around the side.

"It's been another great year for our All Pack meeting," I said quickly, watching as Sam walked over to stand in Anthony's way. "Crescent River Pack will be leaving a little early this year and I wanted to make an announcement before we all head out."

I held my hand out to Hope, smiling as she took it. "Hope and I have been friends for over a decade and we realized on this trip that we are fated mates. I know she means a lot to the Wild Wood Pack, but she has decided to join me as my fiance as we prepare for our mating ceremony."

I kept my eyes on Anthony with the last sentence, his eyes lighting up with rage. A few of Hope's pack members looked surprised, some a little bitter, but most seemed almost... Happy that she was leaving. With the exception of her dad and Anthony, who looked ready to kill.

"It's time to go," I said under my breath. Hope's eyes were glued to where Anthony stood arguing quietly with Sam. He pushed past him as we approached the exit. I pulled Hope back behind me, gritting my teeth as Anthony approached.

"You'll fucking regret this," he spat. "She's mine," he said, looking past me to Hope, "You. Are. Mine." I stepped towards him, growling quietly under my breath.

"She will *never* be yours. Stay the fuck away from us," I turned to Hope, who was focused on Leo and Brianna leaving with a group of pack members in front of us.

"I wouldn't have touched her before, Hope," He continued venomously, "But now? I'll hurt everyone you love before I make you my bitch."

Sam stepped between us as I shifted my claws, my wolf begging to rip him apart. "Not starting a war here, remember?" He said, turning to look at me. "Go cool off Anthony. Half of our pack is here," he continued with a smile, "It's really not great odds for you."

I turned towards the closest entrance, trying to walk off some of my rage. Hope hurried to keep up behind me, her hand gripping mine. We made it to the SUV where Leo was waiting with Brianna.

"Everything okay?" He asked tentatively, looking behind us as if expecting a mob.

"It's fine." I said tightly. "We need to go. Now."

We all climbed in, Hope hesitating even as Leo opened the passenger door for her to sit up front. She climbed in and curled in on herself, staring out the window.

"I'll ride with Sam," Leo said, a knowing look passing between us. I nodded, grateful that he knew we needed some time alone.

After two minutes of driving in silence, my phone finally rang.

"Did you make it out okay?" I asked.

"Oh yeah, Anthony and I are best friends now," Sam joked. "I'm not that far behind you. Everyone else is already on the road, so we are in the clear."

"Thanks for doing that, I'll see you at home." I ended the call, relief flooding through me - we had pulled it off.

The drive continued to be about as lively as a funeral. Hope only looked away from the window to ask how long it would take to get there, while Brianna slept. I tried in the first few hours to talk about what had happened, to see if she had any regrets, but the one word answers told me everything I needed to know. She wasn't ready.

We still had half an hour when my nerves started to get the best of me.

"Are you okay?" Hope asked, her quiet voice a shock after so long in silence.

"Yeah," I said, clearing my throat, "I'm fine. Just mentally preparing. It's not every year I come back from this meeting with a fiance." I joked, hoping to tease a smile out of her.

Her brow furrowed, concern painted across her face. "Do you think they'll be mad?" She asked. I wasn't used to hearing such a timid tone from her, and before I could think it through, I grabbed her hand.

A small zing of electricity ran up my arm as my body responded to hers.

"They won't be mad," I said reassuringly, "Surprised, sure. Annoyed that I waited to tell them until we got home? Most likely, but never mad."

"I know you've met my parents, or at least seen them, at other meetings, but that was in a public place. They are kind of..." I grimaced, "Well, they can be a lot. And I apologize in advance for the absolute freak out they will probably have about you."

We passed the *Crescent River City* sign and turned down the side road that lead to pack lands. Because of the size of our pack, we had more than just houses on pack lands. We had stores, a clinic, and a few other things that made it seem more like a small town than just a neighborhood.

She nodded, drinking in everything outside the window.

"Is something... wrong? I know it may be a little different from what you're used to, I've never been to your pack lands, but we aren't destitute. I just focused on spreading out our wea-"

"No, no, everything is great. Our pack is... very different."

I cocked my head at the bitterness there. She had always kept things about her pack close to her chest when we were kids. Now I wondered exactly how much she hadn't told me.

"That's an understatement." Brianna said from the back seat. I looked in the rear view mirror and chuckled at the rueful smile she had on. "Our alpha had a mansion, and because our father is his beta, our house was decent. Everyone else though? Most of the homes needed fixed up, and if you pissed off the wrong person you could end up homeless."

"It wasn't from lack of working hard, though." Hope said, a fierce, protectiveness emanating from her. "Our pack did the best they could with the people who were in charge. Anthony owns almost everything, everyone rented from him or one of the select few in his council. Even if they had the money, they wouldn't let someone buy anything because it took away their power."

My hands gripped the steering wheel. I knew he was a shit alpha. This wasn't a surprise, and after Elena's vision, I knew there had to be a reason for the prophecy other than he is an ass. But this?

"Our pack isn't like that." I managed to say after a minute, taking deep breaths to keep from clawing the shit out of my steering wheel. "What's good for a pack member is good for the pack." I snuck a look at Hope, watching as she clenched her fists.

"Really? This" She gestured between us, "Starting a war between your pack and Wildwood over some random female is what's best for your pack?"

I had been waiting for this argument. She really had no idea how much she meant to me. And I had no idea how little she valued herself. Someone had done that to her and I would make them fucking pay for it.

"You are not some 'random female'. You're my friend. And, to everyone outside of this car, you're my mate."

# CHAPTER THIRTEEN

## *Hope*

His mate. My mouth was so dry and the knots in my stomach tightened when we pulled up to a house. I couldn't tear my eyes away from the people standing outside of the Subaru parked in the driveway.

His parents and sister. I had seen them at pack meetings before, briefly, but it would have been impossible to forget the only Alpha Pair I had ever heard of. Even if they weren't Jensen's parents.

"Hope?" Bri said, poking me on the arm. "It'll be a better impression if you get out instead of staring at them." I turned and shot her a look, almost smiling at her wide grin.

"They're going to love you," Jensen said, squeezing my hand. "But Brianna is right, we need to actually say hi."

We all got out and I watched as Jensen walked over and wrapped his mom in a huge hug. She squeezed him back just as tight and stared past him at us, curiosity dancing across her features. He let her go and gave his dad a hug as well, reaching out to ruffle his sister's hair when he let go.

"Alright everyone, I want to introduce you to my fiancée," he said, walking over to where I was frozen by the car and grabbing my hand. "This is Hope." I followed after him, my attempts at smiling not reaching my eyes.

His parents looked at each other in shock, their eyes widening. His mom recovered first, shaking her head at him.

"I'm so sorry Hope! Jensen told us he was bringing some new pack members home but we had no idea he was engaged to one of them," she sent him a sharp look as she reached to shake my hand. "I can't believe he didn- " she broke off as soon as I placed my hand in hers, taking a sharp breath.

"Mom?" Jensen touched her arm, looking between us. "You okay?" He said again, looking between us.

She recovered, giving her head a little shake. "Sorry about that! Yes, it is so nice to meet you. I can't wait to hear more about how you and Jensen came together." Her smile was genuine, only a little forced around the edges. She gave my hand a squeeze and released it. I wasn't sure what had just happened, but she definitely was not prepared to meet me.

I glanced at Jensen again, wondering what he had said about us coming back. His eyes met mine and he must have seen my questions there, because he gave a slight shrug. Well, if she wasn't surprised because of him, maybe it was because she knew who I was related to.

A small sigh escaped me. I knew they would have a difficult time adjusting to their son being my fated mate, but I wasn't expecting it to go sideways quite so quickly.

"Thank you Mrs. Valenzuela," I said, pasting on a smile. "Thank you so much for welcoming us into the pack."

"Of course, and please, call me Jenny. This is my husband, Dean, and our daughter, Elena."

Dean stepped forward and shook my hand, his calm smile hiding whatever he was thinking.

"It's nice to meet you both, this is my sister, Brianna." I motioned to her, hoping she was more prepared than I was.

"It's so great to meet you both," Bri bubbled, stepping forward immediately. She had a large smile on her face and looked as if she couldn't think of a better time to meet my future in-laws.

I gave a little shake of my head, turning as Elena stepped forward. "Hi Hope. I have heard so much about you," She said, her bright blue eyes lighting up as we shook hands.

"You have?" I was shocked. When had Jensen talked about me? I looked over at him, just in time to see him frown and shake his head at her.

Turning back to Elena, her grin had widened even more at his reaction.

"You'll have to forgive my big brother, he can be a certifiable asshole sometimes," she joked, reaching out to flick him on the arm.

Jensen rolled his eyes as he reached out and ruffled her hair.

"I am not an asshole. You are just a pain in my ass. There's a difference."

"Why do we keep hearing the word ass, kids?" Jensen's mom asked, turning away from her conversation with Bri.

"I promise, we raised them better," She joked, wearing a pained expression.

"You mean you raised me better," Jensen quipped, "I think you two were worn out by the time Elena came along."

"Real nice," Elena rolled her eyes and linked her arm through mine.

"Come on, lets go inside so you can tell me all about what my brother is like for a mate."

"Okay," I said reluctantly, shooting a panicked look at Jensen. I saw his lips pull down into a slight frown before I turned to go into the house.

I had been so preoccupied when I saw that Jensen's parents were here that I hadn't really looked at the house. Taking the time to really take it in almost stopped me in my tracks.

It was gorgeous. It wasn't pretentious, like Anthony's mansion, and it wasn't overly aggressive, like my dad's. It looked like an actual home. The light yellow made the size seem more homey, and the wrap around porch with flowers planted out front accented that vibe perfectly. I smiled and stopped by the lilies that were closest to the porch, sniffing at the open blooms.

"Jensen and my mom shop for and plant flowers every year on Mother's Day," Elena said with a smile. "This was my parents house when we were all little, so most people assume that my mom is the one who plants them. They have no idea that he's pickier about what goes out here than she ever was. It's been a tradition of theirs since we were kids, in fact," she pointed past me to a climbing rose bush,"I'm pretty sure that he bought that for her when he bought the house."

"That's so... unexpected," I said, my heart softening as I thought of Jensen taking the time to work in the garden with his mom. This was not making the whole platonic thing any easier. I hurried up the steps, taking note of the swing that was identical to the one at the cabin. I stopped at the door, discomfort at walking in first giving me pause.

Elena followed me up the steps, walking around me to open the door.

"It must be odd," she said, "moving in when you haven't been here before."

"It is," I said, hoping that I didn't give anything away. The front door opened up into a bright and spacious living room, with windows that overlooked the front lawn. The light streaming in distracted me initially, until I noticed the bookshelves.

He had at least four bookshelves all on one wall, filled to the brim with different novels. I walked over, reverently touching the books I recognized, restraining myself from pulling out ones I had been wanting to read.

"Jensen has always been a bit of a nerd," Elena joked, her smile widening as I turned around.

"Sorry, I just can't believe how many books he has. And not just a lot of books, but so many good ones!"

"This isn't even half of what he has," she said, smirking. "He has at least this many in his office, and there is a den in the basement with more."

My eyes widened as I considered that. He couldn't have known how much I liked books, there was no way this was staged. He just genuinely wanted to read classical literature, fantasy series, and topics addressing mental health.

Some people think what someone drives can be hot. For me? Give me the contents of their bookshelves any damn day. I reached up to fiddle with my ponytail, turning to the take in the rest of the living room.

"So, do you want to sit?" Elena asked from her spot on the couch. "Or, if you're thirsty, I can show you where the kitchen is?"

"I would actually love some water, if that's alright," I said, my voice scratchy.

"Of course it's alright! Hope, this is your house now too." The panic that had been kept at bay by all of the books I could read reared at that statement. My house? I may be safer in this house than the one I was used to, but it was dangerous in a different way.

Why couldn't Jensen hate books and flowers and also maybe just have inappropriate pin ups on the wall? He could at least try to be a little less attractive.

I sighed and followed Elena into the kitchen, hoping I would hate it and not at all surprised that I didn't. I plopped down on a stool next to the counter while she filled up a glass.

"So, how are you feeling?" Elena asked while I sipped on the water she handed me. "You don't have to talk if you don't want to, but please don't feel like you have to say fine."

My eyes stung at that. "I'm not fine, and I don't really want to talk, but I appreciate it," I said softly, tracing lines in the granite.

Her eyes crinkled at the edges as she gave me a slight nod. "Understood. Well, we can also talk about all the crazy things Jensen used to do. Want to hear about how he used to be convinced he was actually a cat shifter or how Leo and I would prank him?" She asked, waggling her eyebrows.

I laughed at that, some of the pressure easing with her understanding. "Both, lets start with the cat shifter story."

# CHAPTER FOURTEEN

## *Jensen*

"What was that?" I said softly to my mom while my dad helped Brianna grab her bags.

"Nothing, honey, nothing," she said, her eyes darting between me and the house. "She just reminded me of someone, that's all. What did you say her last name was?"

I sighed, knowing that what little time I had hoped for before I had to share this was up. "Her last name is Kelly. She's Jason's daughter."

I turned to her, expecting to see disgust, maybe even anger, at the connection. Neither of those were present. Instead, she was looking at the house with a small smile on her face.

"I knew I recognized her. You know, she's more than just Jason's daughter," she said, giving me a look I couldn't decipher.

"What are you talking about?" I asked, rounding the SUV to

grab the rest of our bags.

"Brianna?" She called out to Bri. "Remind me, what's your mother's name?"

"It was Anna," Bri answered, tilting her head to the side. "Did you know her?"

"Dean and I both did."

"Wait, what?" I asked. "From the meetings?"

"No, I knew her when she was a kid," my mom said, sending a sympathetic smile to Bri. "I was so sad to hear that she passed."

"Thank you," Brianna said softly. "Do you mind telling me about her?" She asked shyly, looking away. "I was only a baby when she died and no one other than Hope ever talks about her."

"Of course we will. How about we go inside so your sister can hear as well." My mom reached over and squeezed my hand as I stared at her. Why had I never known our moms knew each other. More importantly, how had they met as kids?

Those and more questions were racing through my head when we all walked into the house. All traces of them were quickly erased by the sound of Hope laughing from the kitchen.

I listened harder, my smile widening as I made my way in. Hope was sitting at the counter and clutching one of her sides, her other hand wiping away a tear as she gasped for air.

"So then we convinced him that if he really was a cat shifter, he had to use a litter box -"

"Woah!" I interrupted Elena, glaring at her while Hope burst into another round of laughter. "I left you alone with my fiance for three minutes and you start telling her the cat shifter story?"

"Hey, it's comedy gold. You should be proud of yourself, honestly. The commitment it took to scoop your own litter, really. It was commendable," she said, bursting into laughter at my glare.

"If that's the worst she's told her, you should be happy we weren't inside too," my dad said, laughing along with her.

"No more stories about Jensen," I said, grabbing Hope's hand. "Let's go take a tour and get you away from bad influences," I said, shooting my family a dark look that only made them laugh harder. "Traitors."

I led Hope into the hallway with Brianna following closely behind, both of them still chuckling.

"Okay, so our bedroom is upstairs and there is a bedroom downstairs for Brianna that I will show her to in a minute. Do you mind waiting here, Bri?" I asked, ignoring Hope's sudden lack of laughter. I hadn't had the chance to discuss where she would be sleeping.

This was going to be fun.

"I can just go downstairs, you two go get settled in. Which

room is it?" Bri smirked, looking between the two of us.

"Down the hall, first door on the right. It's right across from the bathroom." I said, giving her a subtle nod. She mouthed good luck, covering a snort with a cough as she looked past me to Hope. I bit my lip, trying to hide my smile as I turned to her.

No such luck, she looked two seconds away from attacking me.

"I'm sorry," she whispered. "Did you say 'our bedroom' are upstairs."

Tilting my head towards the kitchen where I knew my family was most likely eavesdropping, I gave a slight shake of my head. Clenching her jaw, she started up the stairs.

Allowing the smile full reign, we made our way upstairs. Technically, there were two bedrooms upstairs.

Technically.

"So, which one is ours?" She asked, practically spitting the words out.

"This one," I said, nodding towards the door at the end of the hallway. She made her way towards it, pausing at the open door of the other bedroom. I shook my head again and pointed downstairs, so she rolled her eyes and kept walking.

She stepped into my, nope, *our* room and turned, pointing to the door as soon as I walked in.

Suppressing yet another grin, I eased the door shut.

"What's up?" I asked, barely suppressing the laugh that was trying to bubble out.

"What's up? What's UP?!" She whisper yelled, pushing the limits of my grin.

"You don't have to whisper up here. As long as you aren't yelling, they won't be able to hear. I made sure there was extra insulation installed in the master when I remodeled."

Her cheeks reddened, whatever she was about to fire back dying on her lips. She looked around, her eyes looking past me to the bathroom door, over to the bookshelf and dresser, before landing on my bed.

Her blush spread down her neck, followed by a glare sent my way.

"Extra insulation? Seriously?" She said, rolling her eyes. "The last thing I need to hear about is all the woman you've been with in here."

"That would be an extremely short list." Really, it would be zero since I moved in, but that was a conversation for another time.

"Sure. Okay. It doesn't matter, we," she gestured angrily between us, "are not really together. Which brings me to my first point, why in the hell are we sharing a room?"

"We aren't really, unless you want to?" I joked. At least, to her.

I'd have her moved in in a second. Quickly followed by us not leaving the room for days.

"Yeah, right." Her brisk tone brought me back to a reality that did not involve us with less clothes on.

"Okay, well for the sake of appearances, you would be sharing a room with me. We are, after all, supposed to be fated mates. Do you really think we wouldn't want to sleep in the same room?"

She glanced at the bed again, her cheeks reddening again. "No. I guess we would."

What I would give to know what thoughts were causing *that* reaction.

"Exactly. So, if it's alright with you, you'll have some of your things in here, but you don't have to sleep in here."

"Okay," she sighed. "Sorry, I guess I should've realized that. I just thought you were trying to force me and I don't take that very well." She glanced down, a frown lingering on the edges of her mouth.

"You shouldn't take that well, Hope. I won't ever force you to do anything. I promise." The fury I had felt over the last several days grew, riling up my wolf. Hope may be safe for now, but Anthony and her father wouldn't let this go.

"I know that we just blew up the tentative peace between our packs and are most likely starting a war because of us." She said, her uncanny ability to read my mind startling me. "Thank you, Jensen," she moved forward, grabbing my hand. "I'm sorry for any future problems this causes, and I will do my best to protect this pack."

I stared at our hands, wanting to pull her in for a hug but knowing it would be best if I let her set the pace.

"Don't you ever apologize to me. Seriously. You are not responsible for their actions, and no one should endure what you did." I stepped forward, allowing myself to put one hand on her cheek as I leaned down. "I would do this all over again even if it ended in a full on challenge from Anthony at the meeting."

She stared at me, disbelief and something else flashing across her face. Giving my hand a squeeze, she stepped away and picked up her bag.

"I should go unpack," she murmured. "Is there a drawer I can use? I didn't bring much with me so I won't need a lot of space."

"I'll clear things out of the top three drawers, there is space in the closet already."

"I won't need three drawers." She said, her voice tinged with embarrassment.

"Maybe not yet, but we have to go shopping this week. You can't live off of a weeks worth of clothes, Hope."

"You don't need to do-"

"The hell if I don't. Either you go with me and get to pick it out or I can go by myself and pick it out for you. You deserve good things Hope. You deserve everything." Feeling like I might do something stupid, like try to kiss her, I turned to leave.

"I'll be downstairs," I clipped out, forcing myself down the stairs.

Pausing at the bottom of the stairs to take a few breaths, I can feel someones stare on me.

"Something on your mind, Dad?" I asked, turning towards the kitchen doorway.

"A whole lot, actually. Why don't you come grab some food and have a chat?" He asked, the casual tone doing nothing to hide the way his eyes were pinched and the set of his mouth.

He was worried.

"You sound completely fine," I said sarcastically, following him into the kitchen. Leo had joined them since I'd gone upstairs and the humor from earlier had evaporated.

"Wow. Full house, huh?"

"Well, we wanted to meet Hope and Elena and felt like it might be good to check in afterwards," my mom said gently, looking past me to my dad.

"That and we all want to know what the hell is going on." It was like Elena to cut through the bullshit. "Hope's awesome, how the hell did you convince her to settle for your ass?" She only sounded like she was half kidding.

"Thanks for your directness, sis. What do you all want to

know?"

"What were you thinking?" My dad blurted, some of the tension breaking through his mask. "The beta's daughter? Do you have a death wish?"

"First of all, she is not the beta's daughter. She has a name, please use it." I clipped out, trying to calm the rush of anger I felt at hearing her connection to that asshole.

My mom moved over to my dad's side, slipping her hand into his. My gaze softened at their affection, knowing that concern was behind the worry.

"Look, I understand this is all... A lot. And there's even more to it than you know, so why don't we all sit down. And maybe have a drink," I suggested, knowing the largest bottle wouldn't make this conversation go over any easier.

"So. What do you already know?" I asked, knowing they would've been talking about this with Leo to gain information.

"Leo hasn't told us much, and your sister didn't have anything else to add. We know you asked about blood magic, which is concerning, and that you are claiming Hope is your fated mate." I bristled at his tone. Thank god Hope had agreed to unpack and decompress upstairs.

"I'm not 'claiming' anything. Hope is my fated mate, end of story. As for the blood magic questions, I'll get to that."

"Jensen. We all know what the prophecy says. Two alphas must rule or both the packs will fail." My dad looked at my mom, who was staring at me. "Maybe I'm missing something, but it looks to me like you're shirking your responsibility. Your mother and I are no longer the alphas. You are. And your fated mate cannot be someone who isn't an alpha."

I stared at the ceiling.

Breathe in.

And out.

That fucking prophecy was going to drive me into an early grave.

# CHAPTER FIFTEEN

## *Hope*

Three drawers. It was such a silly thing, but my heart hadn't slowed down since he told me he was making space for me. Three drawers wasn't even enough to hold all of my clothes back at my house. Not my house, I corrected myself, *Dad's* house. It would take more than a few days to get used to this. I glanced towards the closet, following the shadows hidden there. Without even stepping inside, I was already overwhelmed by his scent. No one should smell that good.

I didn't need to unpack now. Shaking my head, I went to the door. Bri didn't need to spend her time alone, plus she needed someone to take that smirk off her face. Jensen and I were pretending, no matter how much she wanted it to be otherwise.

A sound from the kitchen made me pause on the last step. I knew Jensen's family had stayed, but from the way his voice sounded, it didn't sound like a friendly conversation.

Taking a step towards, I paused as his dad's voice became clearer.

"Your mother and I are no longer the alphas. You are. And your fated mate cannot be someone who isn't an alpha."

Wait.

What?

How could he possibly think his parents would believe we were fated? He had never even seen me shift. God, he had no idea. I pressed a hand to my stomach, hoping to ease the churning within.

"Are you honestly saying you understand the prophecy perfectly? That ANY of us do? It's a fucking prophecy Dad," Jensen growled, the intensity sending bolts of concern through me. "Last I checked, fate has a mind of it's own. She is mine and, alpha or not, she deserves just as much respect and love from this family."

My heart caught in my throat. His sincerity sent my thoughts into a flurry. How could he sound so convincing and be lying? More importantly, how was I supposed to not fall in love with him if he acts like that?

"We aren't going to treat her badly," his mom said soothingly, "it's just that she isn't who we expected you to end up with." I didn't even feel upset by her honesty; I wasn't who I expected Jensen to end up with either. A small wave of guilt settled in my stomach. This wasn't just about us surprising his family, they were genuinely worried about him.

"It's the prophecy that has us worried, son," his dad added. "We already don't know so much about what's going to happen, but this was one thing we did have control over."

Someone started laughing. "Sorry Dad, but isn't fate something that we definitely don't control?" Leo laughed again. At least one Valenzuela seemed happy about us. "Hope may not be an alpha wolf, but she's an amazing person and more than Jensen deserves."

"Really nice," Elena chimed in with a laugh. "Although I don't disagree about her being amazing. Don't mess this one up, okay Jensen?"

My chest warmed at Elena and Leo's defense. Even if this was all fake, it was nice to know I had people in my corner. They probably wouldn't stay there for very long if they knew I was eavesdropping. I started to go back upstairs but the step I was on made the tiniest creak.

I froze, waiting to see if anyone heard it.

"Why are you assuming I'll mess things up?" Jensen asked, sounding irritated. "Everything is going great, but we can all talk more later. I need to check in with Brianna."

Deciding the creak was worth potentially getting caught, I turned to hurry back upstairs when the door swung open.

# CHAPTER SIXTEEN

*Jensen*

Pushing the door open, my eyes immediately found Hope on the stairs.

"When did you come down?" I asked, hoping my tone sounded neutral. She didn't need to hear any of the previous conversation.

"Just now. I wanted to go check on Bri," she said, looking around the room. Her face was completely neutral and didn't give anything away.

"Right." The sound of the front door closing caught both of our attention. The quiet that followed was... uncomfortable.

"Ok -"

"Well -" She finally made eye contact as we both went to speak. The green of her eyes warmed me as I drank them in. A smile tugged at my lips and then fell as her eyes moved to my lips and darted away.

"Sorry, you go," I said.

"I was just going to say I'm going downstairs," she said, turning towards the stairs, "is that okay?"

I winced, hoping she wouldn't keep asking me if things were okay.

"Of course it is, this is you're home now. You can go wherever you want to."

She turned back towards me, her eyes searching mine. Whatever she found there didn't seem to ease her anxiety. If anything, she looked scared as she nodded and left.

"Ahem," Elena cleared her throat, startling me.

"Oh God, Elena, when did you get there?" I asked, putting my hand to my heart. "You scared the shit out of me."

"Wow. Well, hopefully that means you're ready to have an honest conversation. I don't know what I just saw, but it was definitely not two people in love," she probed, raising her eyebrows. "And, for the record, I did not creep up on you. Someone was just a little unaware of his surroundings."

"Was not," I muttered, irritated by the questions. Sighing, I pointed to my office. "Get in."

I looked downstairs, double checking that Hope had gone all the way down the steps, before I followed Elena inside and shut the door. I walked around the desk and sank into my chair. "Okay, ask away."

"And you'll be honest?" she asked, her skepticism rolling off in waves.

"Yep. What's the point in lying? I know you won't tell Mom or Dad, and the ability for you to see the future makes me wonder if you don't already know a little bit."

"I don't. Or, rather, I don't fully understand it..." she said, frustration creasing her forehead. "What I've dreamt makes no sense, but based off of your interaction out there, this isn't a real relationship."

"It is and it isn't."

"Did you even hear how cryptic that was?"

"Yeah, okay, fine. Sorry about that. Hope and I have been circling each other for years. A decade, really. So, in that sense, we have a relationship. Is it a real engagement and are we fated mates? No." As honest as that was, my stomach dropped. We weren't really engaged and we weren't fated mates. She was not going to stick around forever, and I needed to accept that.

"Why the secrets? You knew how everyone would react."

"It's complicated. The short version? Her father was trying to make her mate with Anthony."

"What?" She asked, any trace of irritation replaced by shock. "He's what, twenty years older than her?"

"More like thirty."

"Why would he do that?"

"That's actually part of what I wanted to talk to you about. Did you ever mention the prophecy to anyone other than family?"

"What? No." her eyes widened, "You don't think he knows about it and thinks Hope is an alpha, do you?"

"No. I haven't seen her shift, but even if she was an alpha, they have never had two. And based off of the fact that he was also trying to force her, I doubt he wants a partnership," I ran my hands through my hair and stood up. "I overheard him speaking with their pack witch and he mentioned a prophecy."

"Well, prophecies aren't limited to just one pack. Did he say anything else?"

"Not about the prophecy," I growled, clenching my fists. "He was planning on using blood magic to bind her to his territory."

"I wondered where that had come from. God, that could have been... Disasterous. She could've died before he even got her back to their pack!"

"I know."

"Is that why she agreed to this?"

"No. I didn't need to tell her. I will, there's just been so much going on."

"She needs to know. If he's willing to risk her life just to make sure she stays with him, then this isn't over."

"I know."

"What are you going to tell Mom and Dad?"

"Nothing. I would appreciate if you also said nothing," I said, narrowing my eyes at her.

"I won't. But you have to tell them about Anthony. He isn't going to just let her go."

"I know," I sighed, exhaustion from the past week hitting me, "I will. I just didn't want to go into all of it tonight."

She nodded and shot me a small smile. "I really do like her. You two could be good together."

"I know," I said softly. "I'm just not sure if she will ever see that."

# CHAPTER SEVENTEEN

## *Hope*

Bri didn't have a lot to unpack either, she was reading *Pride and Prejudice* when I came into her room. She smiled when I walked in, looking more at ease than I had seen her all week.

"Have you seen how many books he has?" She asked, her grin widening. "I can't believe it. He has multiple copies of Jane Austen's books!"

I laughed softly, some of my anxiety fading at her joy. I laid down next to her and put my head on her shoulder.

"Which part are you at?" I asked, hoping this peace wouldn't evaporate too quickly.

"Mr. Darcy just insulted Elizabeth at the first ball. He's kind of like the OG Alphahole, you know?" She joked. I rolled my eyes at her.

"Only you would compare Mr. Darcy to an alphahole. Care if I just sit here with you for a little bit?"

"Of course! I'm not going to stop reading though."

"I wouldn't have expected you to," I said, moving my head onto my arms. I focused on my breathing, slowing it down and pausing in between breaths. It's funny how you don't realize how stressful your normal is until you have a new normal. I knew that my dad's house had me on edge, but I really thought it was mostly just when he was home.

Based off of how relaxed I was feeling now, even with all the games and pretending Jensen and I were mates, it must've always been that stressful.

"Hey, I almost forgot," Bri said, putting the book down. "Jenny said that she knew Mom when she was a kid."

"What?" I asked. "That doesn't make any sense? Mom wouldn't have gone to the meetings before she and Dad got married."

"That's what I thought," she said, nodding. "But then I realized I'm not really sure? Dad doesn't ever talk about her parents or really anything about her, so maybe one of her parents took her?"

"Maybe," I murmured, my thoughts turning again to what she would think about all of this. Would she approve? Would she like Jensen?

Hell, would she like me? I stood up, trying to clear my head.

"I'm going to go look at the books in the den and go to bed, do you need anything?" I asked, leaning down to give her a quick hug.

"No, enjoy sharing a room," she said, raising her eyebrows.

"Very funny," I said, turning on my heel. Jensen had rows upon rows of books, with pretty much every genre you could think of. Grabbing a romance novel I hadn't read yet, I sat on the couch and waited until I couldn't hear any sounds coming from upstairs.

When I was sure the coast was clear, I crept up to my room. The light under Jensen's door was on but, thankfully, he didn't come out.

I got ready for bed and laid there reading for a little bit, but my thoughts were too jumbled to focus. After reading the same paragraph three times, I closed the book and turned off the light.

I laid there and thought about how many things had changed in the last twenty-four hours. As much as I was worried about the retaliation my dad and Anthony were definitely planning, I couldn't help but smile at their reaction to Jensen's announcement.

Speaking of situations that sent my thoughts spinning, I had no idea what Jensen really wanted. Why he agreed to this was beyond me. It was even less of a benefit to him than I had assumed; his parents don't think I'm the right fit, there's some kind of prophecy involved, and he's stuck with a shifter who won't shift unless she's alone.

I groaned and rolled over, flipping my pillow over for the cold side. It was easy to admit now, when I was alone and away from him, that I still felt something for Jensen. Seeing all of these glimpses of how he used to be had softened the wall I'd specifically built after him.

And it absolutely terrified me.

# CHAPTER EIGHTEEN

## *Jensen*

My eyes shot open, surprising me. It was still dark out, but something had woken me up. Feeling disoriented, I looked around when I heard whimpering. I sat up and listened harder, my brain still foggy with sleep.

There it was again, a whimper coming from outside of my room.

"No, please!" I heard Hope's muffled voice pleading through my door. My heart jumped as she started whimpering again. I ran down the hallway to her room, ready to hurt whoever was causing her pain.

When I opened the door, it was just her in the room. Her eyes were still closed and she was tossing in her sleep.

"Please!" She yelled this time. "Please, don't leave me!" I hurried over to her, my heart rate slowing.

"Hope," I said gently, touching her shoulder. "Sweetheart, wake up."

She started whimpering louder, her face scrunched in terror. I climbed into bed and pulled her into my arms, hoping that she wouldn't be mad when she woke up.

"Sweetheart," I whispered, holding her and stroking her hair. "It's just a dream, you're safe."

She stopped squirming and froze, her whimper quieting out.

"Jensen?" She sounded close to tears, her anguish still heavy in the air.

"I'm sorry, I heard you and I just wanted to help you wake up," I said, leaning away from her.

"No," she said, turning to look at me with wide eyes. "Please, don't go." I nodded, relieved that she was willing to accept comfort from me.

"Do you want me to hold you?" I asked.

"Please."

"You never have to say please," I said, pulling her back into my arms. "Do you want to talk about it?" I asked gently.

"No." I felt her shudder softly. She clenched her jaw and looked straight ahead. I could see how hard she was working to erect her walls and shut all of that fear down.

"Do you want to lay down or sit up?" I asked, hoping she would want to lay down.

"Let's lay down," she said, sneaking a glance at me. I smiled down at her and laid down, keeping her firmly wrapped in my arms.

"This is new," she said, her voice tinged with humor and something else.

"That it is," I agreed, trying to keep my voice even. She fit so perfectly in my arms, and it was really difficult to not fixate on how perfectly every curve melded to my body. The last thing I needed was to end up hard and for her to notice.

"Tell me something," she asked.

Your ass is incredible.
Nope.
Could we please do this every night until we die?
Definitely not.

I reached up and fiddled with a strand of her hair, taking a deep breath.

"Like what?" I asked, my voice light.

"I don't know. Anything to make me think of something else."

"Well, my mom wants to take you and Brianna shopping tomorrow. Elena will probably go to, so you'll have access to all of the crazy stories about me."

She turned in my arms until she was on her back and could see me. "Any you want to share right now?" She asked, her tone teasing.

"Absolutely not." I said, raising my eyebrows.

She giggled again and my eyes focused in on her lips, on the smile that graced them after she laughed.

"I'm kind of nervous," she admitted quietly. My eyes snapped right back up to hers.

"While the concern you're showing is pretty adorable, it's completely unnecessary. They already love you."

"I'm just not..." She shook her head and started again. "I'm not used to parents being so kind."

My heart ached with rage and pain for her. What I wouldn't give to be able to hurt her dad.

"That makes sense, but I think you'll get more used to it over time. And please, if anyone is not being kind to you, let me know. I'll be more than happy to straighten them out," I said threateningly.

She chuckled and reached up, putting one hand on my cheek. It was the first time she had sincerely touched me just because she wanted to. My entire focus was on that hand and how soft it was, how sweetly she was looking up at me. I just had to lean down a little further and her lips would be right there.

Something in my eyes must have clued her in, because she

moved her hand and looked away.

She turned onto her side, facing away from me. I was about to ask if she wanted me to go but then she scooted back, snuggling right against me. I smiled, then almost groaned as she wiggled a little, her ass rubbing against me.

"Do you mind staying until I fall asleep?" She asked in a small voice, almost as if she was embarrassed.

"I would love to stay until then," I said, taking a chance and pulling her closer to me.

"I wouldn't be against you stroking my hair again," she said with a hint of laugh.

I chuckled and started to stroke her hair again, watching as her eyes grew heavier and heavier. When she had finally fallen back asleep and was snoring quietly, tiny little puffs of air slipping out, I slipped out from her bed and went back to my room.

Without her next to me, it took a long time to fall back asleep.

# CHAPTER NINETEEN

## *Hope*

Sleeping down the hall from Jensen was going to be an exercise in insomnia, even if I wasn't waking up to him comforting me after nightmares. I shook my head at how stupid I felt, my cheeks flushing as I remembered how I asked him to stay until I fell asleep.

Heaving a sigh, I made my way to the bathroom across the hall, hoping I wouldn't see him. His door was open, the bed already made and his room empty.

After using the bathroom, I walked to his doorway and knocked on the frame. "Jensen? Are you in here? I just need to grab some clothes."

No answer. Walking to the dresser, I pulled out my clothes for the day and took a minute to look around. I hadn't had much of a chance before to notice things before, I hadn't wanted him to notice me staring.

His bed was made with hospital corner precision, which made my lips quirk. He was such a perfectionist, I'd forgotten that over the years. I smoothed a hand over his comforter, nodding at how soft it was. Of course he would pick something that felt so decadent, that would make me wonder how soft it would feel on bare skin. Shaking my head, I went to grab the socks I had forgotten when the bathroom door opened. There was Jensen, in nothing but a towel.

"Shit," I stuttered, my eyes roaming from his dripping hair to the water clinging to his six pack. "I, uh, I'm sorry. I just needed to grab some clothes, I thought you were downstairs." God, it wasn't even a six pack. Can people have eight packs? That had to be some kind of extra growth. That was symmetrical. Rolling my eyes at myself, I forced them back to his face in time to catch the small smile there.

"It's not a problem. You've seen me without a shirt on a million times," There was that smile again. "We've been swimming together, remember?"

"We were a lot younger, it was... different," I stopped the word innocent from coming out. This wasn't not innocent. It just felt different because the man looked to be carved out of stone. "I will leave you to it," I said as I turned away.

"Of course," he murmured, the smile in his voice causing the blush that had been fading to come back in full force. Damn if he couldn't still read my mind. Why did I think this would work?

"Hope?"

"Yes," I walked back to the open door, hoping he'd at least put on a shirt.

No such luck.

"Could you shut the door?" He asked, his smile widening as I drug my eyes back up to his for the second time that morning.

"Right, yeah, sorry." Who needs blush when you can't stop embarrassing yourself? I closed the door and fled down the stairs, hoping Bri was awake. Thankfully, I could hear noises in the kitchen.

"Bri, you won't believe -" I stopped, embarrassed when I saw it was actually Jensen's mom. "Sorry, Jenny. I didn't realize you were here."

She chuckled, her eyes crinkling as she smiled at me. "It's completely alright Hope, I came in earlier for coffee with Jensen and stayed so I could check in with you."

"Did you need something?" I asked politely, the conversation I had overheard the night before replaying in my mind.

"It's actually about what you need. I know you left your pack without most of your things. Elena and I want to take you and Brianna shopping for clothes and anything else you may need. Jensen gave us his card to use," she wiggled her eyebrows as she held it up. "What do you say?"

What do I say? I don't even know. I took a sip of coffee, mulling over how to say that I was grateful but also that I didn't want to owe anyone money. Luckily, Bri answered for me.

"We would love that!" Bri said enthusiastically, breezing into the kitchen and grabbing my mug for a sip. "Ugh, why do you drink it without sugar?"

"Because I want coffee, not milk with sugar and caffeine like you drink."

"How does today sound?" Jenny asked, looking at me hopefully. I felt bad for not answering, she was trying so hard to be welcoming.

"Today sounds great, how about after we have breakfast?" I asked.

"Perfect, I will go call Elena and let her know," she turned to leave just as I remembered what Bri had said last night.

"Wait, Jenny, before you go I wanted to ask you about something Bri said. She told me that you said you knew our mom?" I tried to keep my tone even, but the fleeting look of sympathy she sent us showed how well that worked.

"I did, all the kids in our pack went to the same school," she said nonchalantly. "I'm sure you'll run into quite a few people who knew her back then. She also has a cousin-in-law who is her age and still in the pack."

It was as if someone had dumped a bucket of ice water onto Bri and I. We exchanged a look, the confusion I felt mirrored on her face.

"Sorry," said Bri slowly, "Are you saying that she was a

member of this pack?" I watched Jenny as she looked between the two of us, her eyebrows drawn.

"Did you not know she was born into this pack?" Jenny asked softly, her voice full of sympathy. We both shook our heads. Just then, Jensen bounded into the kitchen, his hair still wet from the shower.

"Did you know," I started, my voice cracking. "Did you know my mom used to be a member of your pack?" I asked, hoping he had been in the dark as well.

"She was?" He asked, his shock evident. "I had no idea, did you tell them that, Mom?"

"I thought they already knew, I knew their mom when she was a kid and was talking about how we went to the same school and it all clicked," she said, wincing. "I'm sorry girls, I wouldn't have been so nonchalant about it if I had known you didn't know."

"It's okay. Really, thank you for telling us. Do you think you could tell us more about her?" Bri asked, her tone so hopeful it hurt. I may not have many memories of our mom, but I did remember her. Bri didn't even have that.

"I would love to, but I also think you should talk with Beth. She's the cousin-in-law I mentioned, I'll reach out to her and let her know you're both joining the pack. I bet she'll be so excited!"

"Who's going to be so excited?" Elena asked as she padded into the kitchen with a box of donuts.

"Does no one knock anymore?" Jensen asked grumpily.

"Hey, I brought donuts. Don't complain," she said with a smirk. "Also, pretty sure Dad and Leo just got here too."

"Do I smell donuts?" Leo yelled from the living room. I couldn't help the giggle that escaped at Jensen's scowl. There wasn't any yelling or underlying tension. They just teased and loved each other and I loved it.

I just wished I was actually a part of it.

# CHAPTER TWENTY

## *Jensen*

I watched Hope joking with Elena, her eyes lighting up at something she said.

"Jensen?" My mom said, staring up at me.

"Yeah?" I said, tearing my eyes away from Hope. My mom laughed for a second, looking between the two of us.

"I asked if you needed anything while we were out shopping."

"Nope, I'm good," I said and lowered my voice. "She's going to try to convince you she doesn't need anything. She had a duffel bag, Mom. That's it. And getting the rest of her stuff is not going to be an option anytime soon."

Probably not ever, but you never know.

She looked past me to Hope, her eyes softening. I knew she

would like her, but I hadn't expected it to happen so quickly. I looked at Hope too, grateful that my family was here. If she caught me staring right now, I had an excuse.

I watched as her full lips lifted at something Brianna said, her eyes soft and full of love when she looked at her. God, I wished she looked at me with a fraction of that openness.

Seeming to sense that I was staring, she looked up at me with a question in her eyes. I shrugged, my eyes darting to her lips and back up again. Her cheeks turned pink, making my smile grow even more.

She may keep herself guarded, but those cheeks of hers were a dead giveaway.

"Are you both ready to go?" My mom asked, interrupting our staring contest.

"Yep," said Brianna, "I'll go grab my coat."

"Go where?" Leo asked, reaching for another donut.

"They're going shopping," I said, watching Hope leave the kitchen.

"Oh man, I want to go!" He said, looking at our mom. "I need new clothes, too. Plus, Hope is basically my best friend."

I stomped out of the kitchen, torn between irritation and jealousy. I knew he didn't have feelings for her, but damn if I didn't wish I could call her my best friend still.

Hope, Brianna and Elena were in the living room; Hope was looking through my books, her finger tracing the titles, while Brianna and Elena spoke about what things Brianna wanted to buy.

My parents and Leo came out after me, but I didn't pay attention to what they were talking about. Mates said goodbye to each other and, luckily, my family was around to make sure we did just that.

I walked up behind her, wrapping my arms around her waist.

"See anything you like?" I asked quietly, settling my chin on her shoulder.

She tensed, her hand frozen on the book. I nuzzled her neck, whispering quietly enough that only she could hear me, "They're watching."

She turned and faced me, a small smile on her face. I knew this was going to be difficult for her, but that smile undid me. I moved one hand up to cup the back of her neck and leaned down to press my lips to hers.

She didn't move for a second, her lips frozen under mine. I threaded my other hand into her hair, tilting her head back further so I could coax her mouth open. Her hands moved up to grip the front of my shirt, a tiny moan coming from her when our tongues tangled.

I hadn't planned on doing much more than a chaste kiss goodbye, but that sound and the way she was clutching me sent fire through my blood.

After several seconds, or maybe hours, the hell if I know, I pulled back and put my forehead on hers.

"Are you sure you have to go shopping?" I joked, taking in how the blush in her cheeks had spread down her neck to her chest. It deepened even further when she noticed where my attention had gone, and I looked back up to find her eyes filled with confusion and a hint of lust.

"Okay, okay," My dad said, startling us both. "Let the girl go, you two have your whole lives to do that."

Hope's eyes widened in embarrassment, her nose wrinkling up. I leaned down and pressed a quick kiss to it, her surprise making me laugh.

"I'll see you soon," I said, my eyes glued to her until the car pulled out of the driveway. I turned to see my dad and Leo watching me, wearing the most ridiculous grins. I shook my head, not even a little embarrassed. Fake or not, I wanted to be with Hope in every way that she would allow, and that kiss had been better than I'd ever imagined.

"I need to head out and check in with security, do you need anything before I go?" Leo asked, shaking his head in amusement.

"Nope, I'll call if I do."

I could feel my dad's eyes tracking me as I pulled out the book Hope had been tracing. I read the back, turning to go put it on her bed when I looked up and saw the serious expression on his face.

Shit.

"Is there something I need to be worried about?" He asked, giving away nothing. I wracked my brain, trying to think of if he could possibly know Hope and I weren't real.

"Um.. What do you mean?" I asked, deciding denial would work just fine.

"I noticed last night that we had more guards around the perimeter," he said. The knots in my stomach eased as I realized what he meant.

It was rare for him to question anything that had happened since he and my mom transitioned out of the alpha roles, but based on the wrinkle in his brow, this was the most concerned he had been in awhile.

"Well, I didn't get the chance to go over that with all of you last night. I had Sam get a new rotation worked out with more coverage when we left the All Pack meeting." I walked back into the kitchen, grabbing my mug and taking a sip. He followed with narrowed eyes, something coming together while he leaned against the counter.

"Why do I need feel like there is more to this than Hope just joining our pack?"

"There is. Want some coffee? Mom made it and I have no idea what she did differently, but it's amazing." I was stalling. Every family has their own secrets, their own family members that they don't want to talk about. The ones we don't talk about? Conversations about them ended, at best, with my dad fuming.

"Should I be grabbing some vodka for this coffee?" He joked, his smile tight.

"Maybe," I mumbled, shoving a hand through my hair. "Why don't you sit?"

The apprehension on his face growing, he sat down and took a deep breath. "What is it Jensen?"

"It's about Anthony," I said, wincing at the flash of rage in his eyes. "I know. Worst brother in the history of brothers. This story is probably going to lower your opinion of him further."

"I really don't think that's possible," he bit out. "He hasn't been my brother in a long time, Jensen."

"I know, I'm sorry for the joke. This doesn't have to do with you," I hedged, "Or at least, with your history with him." I walked over to the coffee and continued," It's Hope. Her dad promised her to Anthony, and he was planning on announcing their mating ceremony at the meeting."

I turned around at my dad's sharp inhale. His eyes were wide and his nostrils flared as he opened and closed his fists. "Dad, I know that puts us in a diff-"

"Don't," He bit out, holding up a hand. "I'm not mad at you. She is young enough to be his daughter. And he was going to force her?" He growled now, his wolf's aura filling the room in it's rage. "I am not for one fucking second angry about what you did. Even if she wasn't your mate, I wouldn't question your decision."

Shaking his head, he braced himself against the counter. "I think I will take some vodka in this coffee," he said, clenching his jaw. "I thought he could not sink any lower. I take it you're worried about retaliation?"

I nodded, sliding the vodka over to him. I chuckled as he poured a dash into his cup, took a sip, and added more.

"Hope is our pack now, and more than that, she is my family." He said, jutting his chin out. "She will never be his mate."

I smiled, relieved at how well he was taking this.

"Do you mind going over the new security plan with me? I know you're in charge, it's for my own peace of mind."

I nodded and brought the map we had of the pack lands out.

We reviewed all of the shifts, who was on each shift, and what areas would be easier to target.

By the time we'd gone over ever possible scenario, our coffee was cold and it was almost eleven.

"Have you thought about restricting the access to -?" He paused at the sound of the doorbell ringing.

Having an open door policy during the day meant that pack members came by. Frequently. My phone beeped as the doorbell camera I had sent me a notification. I sighed as I pulled it up and saw who was there.

Lily. She stopped by at least once a week, always with a sense of urgency that didn't quite match the situation. I knew she wanted me to ask her out, but no matter how subtle or direct I was, she was not taking the hint.

I walked over to the front door, pasting on a fake smile before I opened it.

"Lily. What can I do for you?" I asked politely, trying not to grimace at how her eyes roamed up and down my body.

"Jensen," she purred. "I just had a few quick questions about the guard duty assignments. Can I come in?"

I opened the door wider, thankful that Hope wasn't here. The last thing she needed was to worry about Lily.

"I was just going over it with my dad," I said, walking into the kitchen. My dad's eyes widened briefly when he saw who it was, but he quickly masked it with a polite nod.

"Dean! I haven't seen you in ages," she said enthusiastically, her smile wide.

"Yes, it's been a long time," he said politely, looking between the two of us. His eyebrows pulled down as he watched her put her hand on my arm.

I took a step away and pointed to the map. "As you can see, we have a lot of territory to cover." She nodded, her eyes still focused on me.

"What do you need from me?" She asked, her eyes burning into mine. Dammit, I needed to get her out of my house.

"You know, I think Sam has everything all worked out. How about you run over to his house and he can explain it?" I said firmly. When she didn't move to leave, I turned on my heel and walked to the front door. If she wasn't going to take the hint, I'd open my door and shove her out if I had to.

# CHAPTER TWENTY-ONE

## *Hope*

Shopping had gone surprisingly well. They had a mall in town that had plenty of options and we had ended it with lunch from the food court. I couldn't remember the last time I had been allowed to just go out and have fun.

Jenny and Elena had been wonderful and extremely stubborn about buying us clothes. Elena had even tried to talk me into going into a lingerie store. She said she would "rather die" than think about her brother while she was in there, but that everyone needed a few sexy things.

I'd drawn the line at that.

The drive back was relaxed, with Brianna doing most of the talking. That wasn't abnormal for us; I had always been quieter and she seemed to just know what to say to people.

"Thanks again for taking us shopping, this was fun!" Bri said, beaming at Jenny and Elena. I nodded and thanked them again as well. Not being the only one who looked out for us was difficult, and I envied how easily Bri could open up to new people. The front door opened up just as we pulled into the driveway, a tall thin woman saying something to someone inside the house and turning away with a satisfied smile. My throat began to burn as I recognized who those long legs and blond curls belonged to. Lily.

Bri glanced over at me, concern written across her face.

"What is Lily doing here?" Jenny asked, wrinkling her nose as Lily waved at us. She patted her hair and tugged on her shirt, flashing a smile towards us as she went. My cheeks were already starting to burn before she made it to the car, her wide grin showing off her perfectly straight teeth.

"Hi Jen! Elena, how are you?" Her eyes drifted towards the back seat, "Oh wow, I didn't know you were back there Hope! Jensen didn't mention you were coming home so soon," she said sweetly, her fake voice grating on my nerves.

"Hello Lily," Jenny clipped out, a tight smile on her face. "We wanted to take Hope and her sister, Brianna, out as a welcome to the family." Her smile widened as she added, "Just spending some quality future daughter-in-law time."

Elena snorted and coughed in the front seat, looking down as she continued coughing. I hid my smile at their actions, warmth flooding my chest. Sneaking a peak at Lily, I watched as her smile became brittle.

"Of course, that sounds so nice, bless your heart. Well, I will see you all soon, I'm sure." She flounced away, her final comment sending my thoughts spiraling. Why was she even here in the first place?

"Hope," I looked up at Jenny's voice and saw her looking at me through the rear view mirror. "That girl has been chasing Jensen for years and he has not once been interested. Not. Once. Do not give her another thought," she said firmly, waiting until I nodded before she broke eye contact.

Jenny and Elena helps us carry all of our bags into the house, the carefree mood from earlier dampened.

"I'll take my stuff up," I said as I reached for the rest of my bags.

"I can help," Jensen offered from behind me, startling me. I searched his face for any hint of guilt. How long had she been here? Why had she been here?

This isn't a real relationship, Hope. I shook my head, trying to clear the jealousy as we made our way to his room.

"How was shopping?" He asked, putting the bags down on his bed.

"It was fine," I said, turning to stare at him again. Heat flooded me as I noticed the way he stared at my lips, the memory from earlier clearly on his mind. He took a step forward, his gaze never once moving from them, but I didn't want to pretend. Not now, not when she had just been in this house. Had he brought her up here too?

"What was Lily doing here?" I blurted.

"What? Nothing," he said, taking a step backwards as he looked away. "She just had a few questions. It was nothing."

I couldn't take the way he wouldn't meet my eyes, my heart plummeting.

"Okay," I said softly and walked downstairs. I could feel the need to move, to run, building up in me.

"Bri?" I called once I was downstairs, relieved when she popped her head out of the kitchen. "Want to go for a run?"

She nodded, her worry evident as she looked at me and then behind me to where Jensen had just come downstairs.

"Great, I'll meet you outside," I said, hurrying out. The weight eased a little once I was out of the house. I dropped onto the porch swing, moving it absently as I stared out at the street.

A car was slowly driving up, looking as if it was going to pass but it pulled in just as Bri came outside. I couldn't see who was in it, and my apprehension grew. I stood up, moving until I was standing almost entirely in front of Bri.

A woman stepped out, her dark hair streaked with gray. Her eyes immediately found mine and she looked past me to Bri before covering her mouth. She walked towards us and I could see that her eyes were filling with tears.

"Oh my goodness, you must be Anna's girls," she said thickly, a tear spilling out over her cheek. "I'm sorry, it's just that you both look just like your mother." She took a deep breath, gathering herself. "I'm Beth. My late husband was your mom's cousin."

# CHAPTER TWENTY-TWO

## *Jensen*

"Earth to Jensen?" Elena said, snapping her fingers in my face. I pushed her hand away, which just made her smile.

"What?" I asked, shaking my head. Hope had been so quiet, and I couldn't stop myself from wondering why she had looked almost fearful when her sister had asked her to go for a run.

"I have asked you the same question three times, but you've been useless since Hope left." Her smile grew as I rolled my eyes.

"I have not been useless. I was thinking, what did you ask?"

"I asked why Lily was here," she said, narrowing her eyes at me. I tilted my head to the side, confused.

"She came to clarify what time she had guard duty, why?" I asked, wondering why that was important enough to repeat three times. People stopped by all the time, it was one of the more obnoxious parts of being an alpha but it was a point of pride for me as well. Our pack could always come to me if they had questions, and I loved that they seemed to feel just as comfortable doing that with me as they did with my parents.

"Seriously? You sent out an email and Sam sent out texts to everyone about it," she rolled her eyes. "You need to be careful around her."

"Why?" I asked, my mind drifting back to Hope. What had happened on that shopping trip?

"Because she is trying to get between you and Hope, that's why. She's always wanted you to be her mate, and as stupid as she may act, she knows how to manipulate the shit out of people. Be careful around her." I looked at Elena, the seriousness of her tone pulling me back to the conversation.

"Is this a witch thing or just a sister thing?" I joked, knowing she wasn't completely off base. Hope and I had enough obstacles between us already, but I doubted anything could really make the distance more vast.

"Does it matter?" She shot back, poking my in the side. "Whichever one it is, you should listen to me. I know what I'm talking about and I know it's messing with Hope's head."

"Speaking of which, did something happen on the shopping trip? She seemed off when you came inside."

"Have you been listening to me at all? We saw Lily when we pulled in and she made it sound like you two had a private 'conversation' where you forgot to say that Hope would be home soon."

"What the fuck is that supposed to mean?" I asked, a flash of irritation searing my chest. Hope did not need any of that petty shit. Neither of us did. "Is that when Hope started to seem upset?"

"Well," she said, drawing it out. "She definitely seemed to open up more during the trip but she's still pretty guarded. Mom tried to stand up for you and call Lily out on how she was acting, but I can only imagine how it looked to her."

I winced, thinking of what had happened at the meeting. "This isn't the first time something like this has happened."

"What?! I'm serious Jensen, you need to tell that girl to stay away from you."

"You're right. I'll figure something out," I said, turning when I heard a car door shut. "Did Mom leave?"

"Nope, I'm right here." My mom said, coming out of the kitchen. I hurried over to the front door, yanking it open. Beth Andrews was standing there, staring at Hope and Brianna, all three of them silent.

"What's going on?" I asked nonchalantly, moving to hold Hope's hand. She didn't pull away, which after everything Elena had just said, seemed like a small miracle.

"Beth was our mom's cousin-in-law," Brianna said, her voice tinged with awe.

"Your mom was cousins with Ben Andrews?" I asked, trying to think of what Ben looked like. He was a redhead like Brianna.

"She was," Beth answered. "I'm sorry to show up unannounced, it's just that Jenny told me that Anna's girls were joining the pack and I couldn't wait any longer. They look so much like her," she said gently, her eyes roaming over their faces.

I looked down as Hope squeezed my hand tightly. She was still looking at Beth, and while she looked calm, I could tell this was rattling her.

"Why don't you come inside and we can all talk?"I asked, pulling Hope closer to me. She shot me a look of gratitude and leaned into me, her earlier irritation gone.

"I would love that," Beth said, following us inside. We found my parents and Elena in the living room, not even bothering to hide that they had been watching from the window.

"Beth," my mom said, rushing over to give her a hug. "Don't they look like her?" She said, smiling at Hope and Brianna.

"They do," Beth said quietly. I felt Hope tense against me.

It was time to change the subject.

"I had no idea that Anna was a member of our pack," I said, trying to think of a way to move to a different topic. "Who were her parents again?"

"Grace and Thomas Andrews," Beth answered, her eyes glued to Hope's face. "Enough about that, we have plenty of time to catch up. Tell me about how you two met!"

I let out a soft sigh, grateful that she had noticed how Hope had shut down.

"Pack meetings," I said, squeezing Hope. "We'd been friends for years and this year, it just hit that we couldn't live without each other."

Hope moved her arm around my waist, leaning in further. I looked down and caught her staring at me, a small smile quirking her lips up.

"When are you having your engagement dinner?" Beth asked. Hope's eyes widened at her question, a flash of fear dancing across her face before she shut it down.

"I'm not sure," I said, tensing at the mention of it. The last thing we needed was more pressure on us. I looked at Beth and then back down at Hope. She was staring across the room, her face expressionless. "We've had a lot going on, so probably not for a few weeks, at least."

"Well, let me know if you need any help planning it, I would love to do anything I can," Beth offered, concern in her eyes as she watched Hope. Hope looked up at that and sent her a genuine smile.

"Thank you, I'm sure we'll need all the help we can get," she told Beth, her voice subdued.

# CHAPTER TWENTY-THREE

## *Hope*

A soft knock on my door made me bolt upright in my bed. "Come in," I said, my voice scratchy from lack of sleep. Bri poked her head in, her hand over her eyes.

"Is it safe to enter? I don't want to interrupt anything," she joked. I snorted and rolled my eyes, ignoring her. She knew that the last place she would "interrupt" anything was here. A blush crept up my cheeks as I thought about Jensen's disturbingly ridged abs. Nope, not going there. Bri watched me, a knowing smile on her face.

"What?" I asked, irritated at how well she could read me. Because of our heightened senses, shifters picked up in changes in emotions easier than humans, but her instincts were extraordinary, even by shifter standards.

"Nothing," she said, her wide grin saying something else entirely. "Nothing at freaking all. I wanted to check in and see how last night went."

"It went fine. We went upstairs, to our separate bedrooms, and slept. In our separate bedrooms. Nothing is going to happen, you heard him last night. He didn't even want to set a date for our engagement dinner, Bri." I tried to keep the hurt out of my voice. It was fine. He was doing me a favor, that was all. Of course he didn't want to officially announce to his entire pack that he was engaged to someone who was from a different pack and was not an alpha. It would happen, but I didn't blame him for his reluctance.

"I'm sorry," Bri murmured, coming over to wrap me in a hug. It had been an absolute roller coaster of a week, and the comfort in that hug brought tears to my eyes. I wiped them away as we pulled apart, pasting on a smile.

"I'll be fine. It's just been a lot, but it'll be okay. We are safe and together, that's all that matters." I took a deep breath. "Can you do me a favor?"

"Sure, what's up?"

"Can you go make sure Jensen is downstairs?" I asked, hoping she wouldn't ask.

"Uh, why?"

I have none of the luck.

"I need clothes out of 'our' room and I don't want to go in there if he's in there," I tried to keep my voice neutral, she didn't need to hear exactly what I might see. Or couldn't stop thinking about seeing.

Damn that man.

"I guess I can do that," she said, smirking at me. "But you have to tell me what happened after we eat breakfast."

"Nothing happened!"

"Hope, I will go downstairs and leave you stranded up here."

"It was nothing. He is really quiet when he's in his bathroom, he came out after a shower, and no man has real abs like that so I'm pretty sure they are implants. Or some benign growths shaped like an eight pack," I rambled, my cheeks heating.

She rolled her lips in, trying to contain the laughter. "That's nothing, huh? How did the unreal eight pack look?" She asked, her shoulders starting to shake.

"Very funny," I grumbled. "Will you go check or not?"

"Fine," she said as she made her way out to the hallway. "It's clear," she said, chuckling as she came back into my room.

I rolled my eyes at her and hurried out. "Thank you."

"You're welcome," she called after me, still laughing.

I walked over to the dresser and pulled out what I needed, then went into the closet. I paused, listening for anyone on the stairs, but there wasn't a sound. I browsed through my new shirts, finally choosing one and pulling off the pajamas. I'd just pulled on my pants when I heard someone clear their throat.

Dammit.

I turned, my cheeks already on fire. "Jensen. Why didn't you knock?" I bit out, using my shirt to cover my bra. The heat in his eyes as he stared at me sent my blood rushing lower, which only pissed me off.

"It is my closet," he said, his voice sounding as if it was wrapped in silk. "What are you doing in here Hope?" He asked, stepping towards me.

"I was getting dressed, but I can see that this isn't the place for that." I tried to sidestep him  and get to the door, but he frowned down at me.

"Are you angry with me?" He asked.

"Angry? With you?" I asked, sarcastically. "Never." He moved in front of me again as I tried to get past him.

"Why are you angry?" He asked softly, reaching out to tuck a piece of hair behind my ear. I caught his hand, rage pumping through me.

"Why am I angry? Should I list it alphabetically or sequentially?" I said, his smile at my comment making me angrier. "Let's start with you and Lily, who are 'not' a thing. Funny how she keeps showing up and having one-on-one time with you."

"Are you jealous?" He asked, taking another step forward.

"Jealous?" I sputtered, my voice getting higher. "Over our fake relationship?"

"We may not be real mates, but that doesn't mean there isn't something here." He said, moving forward again. I took a step back this time, my back bumping into a shelf.

"Something here, huh? Funny, you'd think that if there was something, you would want to have our engagement dinner." I said, poking him in the chest.

"Who said I didn't want to have it?" He asked, surprise mixing with the lust in his eyes.

"You did!" I yelled, exasperated. "You said it last night. So," I spat, stepping forward until our chests were touching. "As much as you act like this is 'something', we both know that's bullshit," I said, jutting my chin forward.

His eyes roamed over my face, settling on my lips. He leaned down to my ear "You know what I think?" He whispered. "You're scared." He pressed a soft kiss to the skin under my ear, a small shiver going through me.

"You're attracted to me," he said, kissing my neck again and then nipping at my earlobe. I gasped softly, making his lips curve up against my neck. "And it terrifies you."

# CHAPTER TWENTY-FOUR

## *Jensen*

My heart was pounding so loud that I couldn't even hear hers. Her hands that had been gripping my arms moved quickly as she pulled my face away from her neck and up to hers.

Her lips were urgent against mine, her teeth almost drawing blood as she sucked in my bottom lip. I groaned and pulled her leg up to my waist, wanting her to feel how hard I was. She rocked against me, using her leg to pull us closer together.

I grabbed her other leg, pulling both up to my waist and holding her tight ass. Turning, I pinned her to the wall, my hands moving back up her body.

She was panting as I pulled away from her perfect lips, my mouth trailing kisses down her neck to her chest. She'd dropped the shirt while we were arguing and I could see how hard her nipples were through her bra.

"Do you want me to kiss you here?" I said huskily, trailing my hand just above her bra line. She moaned softy, nodding as she closed her eyes. I smiled, pushing her bra down until her beautiful tits were exposed. I covered one of her nipples with my hand, plucking and rubbing it while I took the other in my mouth. Her back arched as I flicked at it and sucked, her moans driving me to distraction.

"Jensen," she panted, scratching the back of my neck. My name on her lips like that was enough to make me combust. I started on the other side, my teeth scraping her nipple as she held me closer.

She pulled me away just as her moans were getting louder, guiding me back up to her mouth. Our tongues tangled and I pushed in closer to her, rubbing her along my cock.

"Just like that," she panted, tilting her head up as I moved faster.

"Do you want to come, baby?" I asked, leaning down nip at her ear. I laughed as she nodded, her hands pulling me closer. I turned and put her on the shelf in my closet, her legs still wrapped around my waist.

"I bet you're soaked," I whispered in her ear, smiling as she nodded. I reached down to her waistband and paused, leaning back to see if she was okay. She grabbed my hand and put it on the button of her jeans, her eyes blazing.

That was enough encouragement for me.

I unbuttoned them quickly, kissing her deeply as I did. "Baby, your underwear is soaked," I groaned, moving them to the side. She pulled me closer as I stroked her clit, her breath coming faster as I put a finger inside of her.

I eased another finger inside, using my thumb to put pressure on her clit.

"Right there, oh my God," she panted, her hips moving with my hands, "Please Jensen," she pleaded. I watched as she rode my fingers, her flushed cheeks and moans sending me almost to the edge.

"Come for me baby," I panted, completely undone as she clenched around my fingers, moaning my name.

I took my hands out of her tight little pussy, making eye contact as I sucked on my fingers.

"God, I could live off of how you taste," I purred. Her eyes widened as she watched me, some of the heat returning. I reached over to fix her clothes and surprised her by picking her up.

"What are you doing?" She asked, flustered.

"What can I say, I'm a cuddler," I said, laying her down on my bed. She chuckled and moved over close to me as I laid down next to her. I pulled her into my arms, struck again by how perfectly she fit.

I held her like that in silence for a few minutes, until her body began to tense and I could feel her worrying about something.

"What is it?" I asked, turning her around.

Her brow was scrunched and she looked as if she was holding back tears. "I can't.. I can't be who you need me to be," she said softly, looking away from me.

"I don't need you to be anyone, Hope. Just you."

She took a deep breath, steeling herself. "I'm not an alpha, Jensen." She said, her voice colder.

I froze, staring at her in shock. "Why does that matter?" I said, my mind racing as I tried to think of how she knew about the prophecy.

"I heard you the night we got here," she said softly, sitting up. "I don't care if we fool around sometimes, but I can't be your real mate." She stood and walked into the closet.

She came back out with a shirt on and her face completely closed off. "I know you haven't seen me shift, but you never will. I love my wolf too much to put up with another person telling us we don't measure up." The finality and pain in her tone gutted me.

I watched her walk out of the room, my thoughts completely jumbled. I couldn't believe someone had ever made her feel ashamed of her wolf, even though it seemed pretty par for the course with her dad.

How do you convince someone that they are more than enough when they've been told the opposite their entire life?

Another thought struck me. Why did her saying she couldn't be my mate devastate me?

# CHAPTER TWENTY-FIVE

## *Hope*

"Do you want some tea?" Beth asked. I looked up from the pictures on her walls, disoriented. I'd been avoiding Jensen and, thankfully, Beth's house was a safe place to do that.

"Yes, please. Thank you for letting me come over for the last few days," I said, walking over to her kitchen counter.

"Of course! You're family, and I'm sure it's been a huge transition. Living with your mate for the first time is a pretty big step," she said, sending a knowing smile my way. My cheeks heated as I thought about the last time I had been in a room with Jensen for more than a minute. I couldn't believe I'd let it get that far. Or that I'd told him about my wolf. I let out a groan and put my head in my hands.

"You have no idea," I mumbled, trying to pull it together. I hadn't told Beth that Jensen and I were faking, but I wondered if she had an idea something was going on. She hadn't said anything outright, but some of the things she said made me think she knew.

She chuckled, bringing over a basket with tea choices and a mug.

"I know how hard it is to have someone else in your space," she said wistfully, her eyes going to a picture of Ben on the wall. "As difficult as it is, I'd go back to those days in a heartbeat."

"Oh god, I'm so sorry Beth," I stumbled on my words, "I shouldn't complain. How long has he been gone?"

"Three years," she said, shooting me a sad smile. "Don't apologize. I miss him and you're having a difficult time adjusting to your mate - those things can coexist without me feeling hurt."

I stared at the picture on the wall, realizing for the first time that he had the same color eyes as my mom.

"He looks like her, doesn't he?" She asked softly.

"He does," I agreed, "I don't have any pictures of her. My dad... He didn't keep anything and her eyes are the only thing I remember clearly. Brianna has the same eyes." My heart ached as I stared at Beth. If only I'd come here sooner, if only I'd known that she belonged to another pack.

"I have pictures of her, if you'd like to see?"

"You do?" I asked, eagerness and shock overwhelming me.

"Yes, I can even make copies of everything for you and your sister, if you'd like?"

"I would," I stopped, my throat thick. "I would love that, thank you."

We went to the living room while my tea steeped and settled onto the couch. Beth went over to a shelf that had multiple photo albums and pulled three down.

"I know she is in at least two of these, maybe all three. My mother-in-law was big on family pictures," she said, passing the first album to me and sitting down.

My hands trembled as I looked at the cover photo. There were so many people in it, mostly adults with a few kids running around. Beth pointed out a scrawny teenager with his arm around a younger girl, both of them laughing. "There they are," she said softly. "They used to have a huge family barbecue every year, I think this one was almost thirty years ago." I nodded, not trusting my voice as I drank her in. I hadn't realized how much Bri looked like her; they had the same nose and curly red hair.

"You have her smile," she said, looking back and forth between the pictures. I opened up the pages, every new picture of her bringing wave after wave of emotion. I paused as the tears started to fall, not wanting to risk any of the page protectors getting water in them.

Beth handed me tissues from the table next to her and put her arm around me.

"Thank you," I said thickly, dabbing at my eyes.

"Anytime sweetheart. I'm so sorry that you didn't know about us this entire time."

I cleared my throat and looked at her. "I've been wanting to ask you about that. Do you know why my mom left the pack?"

Beth winced and looked down. "I do," she murmured, looking back at me with tear filled eyes. "It's not a happy story, Hope."

The urge to burst into laughter was almost too much. "Trust me, I'm more than aware of how this story ends. It was never a happy one for me."

"You're right, of course. Well, your mother and I were friends before I married her cousin. She's actually how he and I met, but that's a story for another time. When we were 17, she met Jason at the All Pack meeting." She narrowed her eyes as she said my father's name, a look of disgust flashing across her face. "Meetings back then were different. We had four packs in the area then and it was always so fun. There wasn't any tension or different designated areas for each pack. We all mingled and bonded for an entire week."

She took a deep breath, her eyes distant. "Your father seemed so sweet. Too sweet, now that I look back on it, but at the time, he seemed perfect. Your grandma had passed away the year before, and your grandpa had started to drink heavily. Your mom didn't have much to look forward to at home, and someone who was willing to pay attention and shower her with love? It seemed like a dream. She soaked up all of that attention and fell fast."

My heart broke a little as I imagined what that must have

been like. I knew far too well what it was like to have an alcoholic father and a dead mother.

"They kept seeing each other on the weekends after that and one day, when we were seniors in high school, she told me she was pregnant."

"Wait," I said, shock flooding me as I did the math. "That wasn't me. She had another baby?"

She shook her head, her jaw clenched. "No, she didn't. When her dad found out she was pregnant, he was furious. He kicked her out and told her to stay away. Jason told her how excited he was, said they should have their mating ceremony. Why wait when they already were having a baby?" Her face fell and her voice trembled. "I had been worried about their relationship, but when he wanted to get married, I finally said something. She was upset and told him what I said. He was furious and told her she shouldn't talk to me anymore, that I was trying to break up their family." She let out a humorless laugh. "He played the part perfectly, and she left. She called me for the first time three months later. They were married and he had let his mask slip as soon as it was official."

She swallowed hard, tears filling her eyes as she looked back up at me. "He got drunk one night and pushed her down the stairs. The baby didn't make it." She reached for a tissue and choked back a sob. The numbness in my chest spread, tamping down the rage I knew would come back later.

"I'm sorry, I know this must be so hard for you to hear," she said, taking deep breaths to stop her tears. "Your mom was the closest friend I ever had and she just had one awful thing happen after the other. She didn't deserve any of it."

"No," I said woodenly, staring at the ground. "She didn't." I pushed up off of the couch, feeling dizzy and like I needed to move. "I need to go," I blurted out, moving towards the door.

"Of course," She said, the concern in her eyes boring into my back. "I'll make copies of these for you and get them over as soon as I can."

"Thanks," I said, my chest tight. I almost ran to the door, my breath coming in gasps.

I rushed down the sidewalk trying to shut down my emotions, panic starting to take over when I couldn't get enough air. I sat with my back to Beth's fence, putting my head in my hands.

My breaths eventually slowed, but I knew I needed to talk to someone. Pulling out my phone, I called Bri. I focused on the rings while I continued breathing in and out slowly. A small jolt of panic raced through me when it went to voice mail.

I tried again, fear really setting in as it went to voice mail a second time. I sent her a text, telling her to call me when she saw this. I wracked my brain, trying to think through the panic. She had said she was going to go for a walk down by the river earlier, but the house was closer to me.

I needed help.

I needed Jensen.

# CHAPTER TWENTY-SIX

## *Jensen*

"Jensen? Are you in here?" Hope's voice was frantic, the front door slamming shut behind her. I ran towards the living room, concern racing through me.

"Are you okay? What happened?" I ask, my eyes checking all over her for signs of injury.

"It's not me, it's Bri. I can't find her and she isn't answering her phone. She left earlier and said she was going for a walk by the river and now I can't find her." Her hands started to shake as her voice rose, panic lacing every word. I pulled her to me with one arm, pulling out my phone with the other.

"It'll be okay. I have a guard with her, let me call him and see where they are." I said, tamping down my own concern as I rubbed her back. I dialed Sam, holding my breath while it rang.

"Hey man, what's up?" Sam said, sounding completely at ease.

"Who has Brianna right now?" I asked, trying to sound serious but not worried. Hope watched the phone, straining towards it as if she would be able to hear her sister.

"It's actually my turn right now. She walked over to the park. Do you need her back home?"

I inhaled sharply, smiling down at Hope as she closed her eyes in relief.

"No, we were just worried. Could you tell her that Hope has been trying to call her and to text her or something when she has a minute?"

"Do you care that she'll know I'm watching her?"

"No, I'm starting to think maybe we should all be aware that guards are around." Hope laughed shakily at that, walking over to the couch and sinking into it with her head in her hands.

"Okay, I'll let her know."

"Thanks Sam, I'll see you later." Ending the phone call, I turned to see Hope's shoulders shaking as her breath came in small gasps. The ache in my chest grew, causing my own eyes to water as I sat down next to her and began rubbing her back.

"Hey, what is it?" I asked, leaning down to kiss her on the top of her head.

"I'm sorry," she said, sniffling. "I was just so scared and I'm pissed at myself. I can't believe I didn't keep her with me. I know how crazy my dad and Anthony are. I know how much danger we're in, and it's my fucking job to keep her safe." She lifted her head, tears tracking down her cheeks. "Thank you, by the way. I can't believe you've had a guard on her this entire time."

Moving down to my knees in front of her, I cupped her face. "You don't need to thank me. You're both my family now, and I will always keep you safe."

She closed her eyes and gently nodded, her tears starting to slow. Even as they slowed, the pain on her face didn't ease.

"Is something else wrong?" I asked, my voice gentle.

"I was with Beth earlier and she told me why my mom left. I knew it couldn't be good, it's not like he ever treated her well when I was alive, but I think a small part of me hoped that he had at one point treated her like she deserved," her voice broke, "It was worse than I imagined."

I grabbed tissues and brought them over to her, my absolute rage at her father raging alongside the helplessness I felt. I sat next to her, hoping just being close would ease some of the hurt. "Would it help if I held you?" I asked, at a loss for what else to do.

She nodded, her face crumpling as she leaned into me. I pulled her into my arms and held her, tears welling in my eyes as she sobbed. I rubbed her back as we sat there in heavy silence. Her breaths slowed, but she didn't move away.

"I don't know how to do this," she whispered, looking up at me with wide eyes. "I don't know how to just be and not worry this is all a lie."

My breath caught in my throat, hoping she was talking about more than just faking our relationship.

"When you say 'this' do you mea-" My phone ringing made us both jump. Hope stood up and walked to the window, wiping her eyes as she went. I clenched my jaw and answered the phone.

"I hope you have a really good reason for this call," I bit out.

"I do," Sam said, his voice tight.

"Someone found a dead guard."

# CHAPTER TWENTY-SEVEN

## *Hope*

"Where?" Jensen barked out, his jaw clenching. I'd moved far enough away that I couldn't hear whoever was on the phone, but I could feel the tension. "Fuck," he muttered. "I'll be right there. Call my parents and siblings. I want three more guards sent to that area and whoever the fuck is watching the security cameras better have something for me when I get there." Jensen hung up the phone and pinched the bridge of his nose.

"What happened?" My apprehension was growing; whatever it was, I could feel his wolf pushing on mine, his anger palpable.

"We need to go down by the river. Someone found a pack member's body."

"What?" I yelled, fear flooding me as I remembered where Bri had wanted to go. "Who?"

"It's not someone you've met yet. He's one of our guards," he bit out. He took a breath as if he was going to say something but thought better of it. "We can talk more once we get there, but we need to go now. Sam is bringing Brianna to the area so we can all be together and find out what happened."

I nodded, hurrying over to grab both of our coats. Jensen went down the hall and came back with a hunting rifle, his jaw set. I handed him his coat and followed him out to the car, noticing the tension in his shoulders.

I couldn't shake the feeling that this was because of me.

The ride to the river was quick, but there were already several cars there. Bri was standing with Sam and Elena, her face pale. I ran out as soon as the car was in park, throwing my arms around her.

"You always answer the phone," I said, leaning back and grabbing her arms. "Always! And if you miss it for some godforsaken reason, call me back." I pulled her back into a hug, closing my eyes.

"I'm sorry," Bri said, her voice muffled. I stepped back and she looked down sheepishly. "I didn't realize it was on silent." I shook my head, a small smile turning my lips up for a second before I remembered why we were here. Sam had moved over by Jensen and his parents and was speaking in a low voice I couldn't hear. Suddenly they were all turned to us, his parents faces paling and Jensen looking like he was going to tear someone apart.

"That doesn't look good," Bri murmured. "Oh!" She exclaimed, her eyes turning to her wolf's yellow. Before I had the chance to ask what she was feeling, Jensen was there and putting his arm around me.

"I need you and Bri to go home," he said, his tone severe as he steered me towards the car. "I'm sending you with Sam and we will have more guards posted outside of the house."

"Wait, what? What's going on?" I asked, digging in my heels. I dipped out from under his arm and whirled around. "Who is in those woods?"

"No one you know," He ground out, his eyes flashing angrily. He reached for my hand, but I stepped back.

"Jensen," I growled. "What the fuck is going on?" Jensen clenched his jaw and pushed a hand through his hair.

"Brianna, I need you to go wait in the car," he said gently, turning to Bri.

"The hell I am," she fired back, jutting her chin out. "I'm almost 18, Jensen, and you are not in charge of me." He turned to her, his eyes widening.

"What exactly do you think being the alpha means?" He said, his voice thick with amusement.

"I'm in charge of you, Bri, get in the car," I said, knowing that whatever had happened wasn't something she needed to hear right now.

"Seriously?" She griped, trudging towards the car. "I'm practically an adult, this is ridiculous," she muttered under her breath, climbing in the backseat and slamming the door.

"One down, one to go," Jensen said, reaching for my hand again. I let him grab it this time but yanked him towards me.

"What. Happened?" I clipped out. Jensen's eyes searched mine, fear flashing through them as he looked past me into the woods by the river.

"The guard we found? He was the one who was with Bri earlier today. He switched shifts an hour before I called Sam." Ice flooded my veins. This wasn't just about someone being killed. I turned to look at Bri through the window, fear and rage warring in my chest. They'd come for my sister. They'd killed a member of my pack.

"Hope," Jensen said gently. I turned back to him, my wolf clawing at my skin to shift, to tear apart whoever the fuck thought they could hurt my sister. Kill a member of my new pack. "I need you to go back to the house where it's safe."

"Like hell I am!" I yelled, feeling my rage grow. "They want to come for me? I will rip them apart." I said softer, my voice like ice.

"No, Hope. I can't have you here. I can't focus when I'm worried about keeping you safe," he pleaded, grabbing my other hand. I wrenched them free, irritation flashing through me.

"I'm a big girl Jensen, you don't get to decide what I do."

"I know, I know I don't. I just," he blew out a rush of air and gripped the back of his neck. "This isn't about your abilities. It's 100% about my fear, I know that. Please, just for tonight, will you go back with Bri?"

"Fine." I said, grinding my teeth. "We'll talk more about this later. Something tells me the alpha's mate shouldn't be sitting on the sidelines."

He stepped forward in a flash, one hand around my waist and the other gripping the back of my neck. "That's the first time you've called yourself my mate when we're alone," he said, his eyes darkening. Before I could even take a breath, he leaned down and pressed his lips to mine.

His hand tilted my head back further as I opened my mouth to him. Our tongues clashed, the kiss deepening. He pulled away and pressed his forehead to mine as we caught our breath. "Please. Stay safe." He murmured, pressing a kiss to my forehead. I nodded mutely and climbed into the SUV. Sam looked over at me and took in a breath to say something, but let it out when I shot him a look.

"Message received," he said with a nod. "Let's get you two home."

# CHAPTER TWENTY-EIGHT

## *Jensen*

I stood and watched until Sam had driven out of sight. A small measure of relief came from them going home and away from this. I strode back over to my parents and sister, listening to the conversation my brother was having on the phone a few feet away.

"Okay," Leo said, putting his phone on speaker. "I've got the rest of us here now, Jake. What do you got?"

"Unfortunately, not a whole lot," Jake said warily, "Whoever did this knew we had cameras on that part of our border. They were driving a black SUV with tinted windows and the license plate covered up. Three people exit the vehicle, three people come back. They're wearing dark clothes and their faces are covered."

"Dammit," I muttered, my irritation growing. I didn't think we needed any evidence of who did this, not really, but it would be nice to have concrete justification for the war I was ready to start.

"How did they get past the fence for that road?" My mom asked, her brow furrowed. I'd completely forgotten that road had a fence, it was a part of the pack's property and was kept gated year round.

"I checked the cameras over there as well and the gate was unlocked," Jake answered, sounding confused. "I know quite a lot of people have access to that key, but we all know to keep it locked."

"Maybe it wasn't an accident," Elena suggested darkly. As much as I didn't want to believe someone would be working with Anthony's pack, there were too many coincidences. How did they know who had Brianna? Or where she had been earlier that day?

"Jake, can you go through footage and see when the last time was that someone unlocked it?" I asked, trying to remember who had access to the gate. Sam would know, he was over our security and kept records of things like that.

"Sure, but it may take me a few days. We have no idea how long it could've been that way."

"That's fine, have the rest of security take shifts reviewing it. You don't need to be glued to a screen for days." I said.

"Will do. Good luck over there."

I looked over to where our pack doctor was examining the body. I braced myself as I walked towards him. Sam hadn't said how he died, but I had known Zander since we were kids. This was going to hurt.

Dr. Hansen was crouched down next to Zander, taking off the gloves she was wearing. She stood up as I approached, her expression somber.

"It was a gunshot, silver bullets," she said gently, "He would have gone fairly quick."

"Thank you. I'll take it from here," I said, wanting to be alone to examine the body. Xander was several hundred feet away from where he was supposed to be, and based off of the footprints to this area, he hadn't been chased or in a hurry to get over here.

I walked past him over to the trees bordering the river. There were conflicting scents, but they all had one thing in common. They were Wildwood Pack.

"What do you got?" Leo asked, his face pale as he walked towards me.

He and Xander had grown up together.

"You don't have to look at this right now," I told him firmly, putting a hand on his shoulder. "Seriously, why don't you go see the Williams? They know you best."

He nodded as he looked down at the muddy bank. "Fine. Once I do that, I'm helping you. I need to feel like I'm doing something."

"Alright. Let me know if you need any help talking with them."

He turned and left, his steps a little unsteady. I pushed my hand through my hair and turned back to the trees. It looked like they had shot him from over here, but why? No one else was around, why would they shoot him if he wasn't even guarding Bri?

It didn't make any sense and I couldn't shake the feeling that this had gone exactly as Anthony wanted it to.

"Jensen!" A voice yelled. I looked over by my parents and saw Xavier standing there, peering past my parents to where his brother's body was.

"Shit," I muttered. I walked over to where he was, my parents both trying to talk to him. His eyes had shifted to his wolf's yellow and he looked two seconds away from having a complete meltdown.

"Jensen," he said, relief lacing the words as he saw me walking up. "What happened?" He asked, his voice trembling.

"We don't know yet Xav," I said gently. "Wait, how did you know what happened? Leo just left to tell your family."

"I felt him earlier. He was in so much pain, I couldn't take it," He said in a rush. "I knew he was on guard duty today with your mate's little sister, but I didn't know where, so I followed his scent and tracked him here."

I glanced at my parents, worried when I saw they were

surprised too. I had never heard of someone feeling how another shifter felt. Not like this, not where there was distance and they couldn't use their physical senses.

"Can I go see him?" Xavier asked quietly, his voice wavering.

"Yes, of course. We have to keep our distance until forensics comes, but you can see him."

We walked over to Xander's body, Xavier's sharp inhale burning my throat. He let his tears fall, unashamed, as he knelt down on the ground.

My rage returned in full force. "I'll find them," I told Xavier. "I'll find who did this and they won't live another fucking day."

# CHAPTER TWENTY-NINE

## *Hope*

I rolled over to peek at Bri, happy to see that her eyes were still closed. Relief flooded my chest as I thought about how close I'd been to losing her. I slowly crept out of her bed, silent as I crossed to the door. We had been up late talking about what happened and she needed to sleep, it was too early for her to wake up. She also had a lot of questions about the kiss she saw that I did not want to think about this early.

I had a lot of questions too.

My thoughts turned to Jensen as I made my way upstairs. I hadn't heard him come home last night, but I could smell coffee coming from the kitchen. I walked in, hoping he would have more news but was disappointed when I saw Sam standing there.

"Good morning Hope," he said on a yawn, sending a smile my way.

"Morning Sam," I said quietly, searching for a mug from the cupboard. He passed the coffee pot to me and started sipping on his own mug filled to the brim. Based on the shadows under his eyes, it looked like he had been awake all night.

"Have you slept yet?" I asked, concerned. He shook his head and hid another yawn. He pulled out his phone and checked it, his brow furrowing.

"I haven't, but I'm about to trade out with Beth. I'll go get some sleep and meet up with Jensen after that."

"Oh, has he not come home yet?" My voice had gotten higher, more worry there than I felt comfortable with. "Have you heard from him?"

Sam's eyes softened as he looked at me, an understanding growing in them as he cocked his head to the side. "You really love him, don't you?" He asked, a smile spreading as I choked on the drink I was taking. He chuckled as I continued coughing, shaking his head. "You two are better than a reality show, I'll give you that. Yes, I heard from him, he's been out all night." His face darkened and he looked away. "He had a lot to do last night, I'd be surprised if he was home before noon."

I coughed again, trying to clear my throat. "Thank you for letting me know," I said, avoiding his earlier comment. "I need to get out of the house, will you tell Bri that I went for a walk?"

He nodded, his eyes still probing. "I will. Don't forget that a guard will be following you."

"How could I?" I asked with a sigh. I put the mug in the sink and ran upstairs to change. I avoided looking at Jensen's perfectly made bed as I pulled out new clothes. I changed quickly, brushed my teeth, and hurried outside, looking forward to feeling the sun on my face.

Three guards were standing at the front of the house, with another parked in a car. I nodded to them, recognizing one who had been at the river the night before. After a quiet conversation between the four of them, the one I recognized walked over.

"Hi Hope. I'll be your shadow today," he joked, a small smile playing at the edge of his lips.

"Awesome," I said shortly. Logically, I understood why Jensen wanted someone to stay with me. I was even happy about someone staying in the house when Bri was there, but I just wanted to be alone and not worry about how I acted or what I said.

I started walking down the street, expecting the guard to stay behind me. Instead, he fell in to step next to me, stealing a glance at me every block or so. After five minutes of this, I'd had it.

"Did you want to say something?" I asked, my voice flat.

"Oh, sorry. I just... I was just wondering, is it true your dad is the beta for the Wildwood Pack?" He asked, his voice curious.

I stopped walking, surprised. I assumed he was going to ask about Jensen, or even about what I had seen last night. This was... unexpected.

"Um, yeah. He is." I said awkwardly. "I'm sorry, I'm not trying to be rude, it's just been a really tough twenty-four hours."

"It's okay," he said. We walked in silence for longer, aimlessly wondering through the side streets.

"Hope?" I felt myself tense as Lily called my name. What are the fucking odds? She was everywhere.

"Do you think I can pretend we didn't hear her?"I muttered to the guard. He snorted and shook his head.

"I can tell her to fuck off though, if you want?" He suggested back.

"Probably a bad idea," I said, turning around to see her walking up.

"It is you! That black hair of yours stands out like bruise," she said sweetly, her smile widening as my fake smile slipped. God, she was just the worst.

"Yep, that's me." I said flatly. The guard looked between us, his eyebrows raised.

"Did you need something?" He asked brusquely, his irritation comforting me.

"No, I just wanted to apologize to Hope for keeping Jensen out so late," she said, her eyes widening innocently. "I know he had so much on his plate after Xander and I just wanted to help him feel better."

Feel better? I kept my face straight as rage enveloped me.

"It's no problem," I replied, my tone as sweet as hers. "Anyone who wants to help my mate is a friend to me," I shot back as I turned away. It was probably not the most graceful exit, but short of telling her to fuck off, it was the best I could do.

Anger made the walk back to the house go by quickly, and gave me time to figure out my plan.

I had to leave. I could stay in the pack, but there was no way in hell I was staying with Jensen.

# CHAPTER THIRTY

*Jensen*

I walked up to the house, relieved to see all of the guards posted that should be there.

"Are they both inside?" I asked Beth wearily. I'd been up for thirty hours and was more than ready to crash.

"Yes," she said, hesitating. "They are." She eyed me, pausing before she continued. "You might want to check in with Hope before you go to sleep."

"Did something happen?" Fear rose as I strode up the steps, not waiting for an answer. No one was in the living room, and I couldn't hear anyone on the main floor so I headed for the stairs.

"Hope?" I called, taking the steps two at a time. Relief flooded me as I heard her voice, low and irritated. Confusion followed as I realized she was muttering to herself in my room while she emptied her drawers. She turned to me when I came into my room and quickly looked away, but not before I saw the anger there.

"What are you doing?" I asked, bemused.

She froze, her hands full of her clothes as she turned to me. The rage there made me take a step back - she looked two seconds away from throttling me.

"What am I doing?" her voice trembling with barely suppressed rage. "I am packing, Jensen. Give me a minute and I'll clear my new clothes out of the closet and be out of your hair."

"Wait a minute," I said, crossing over to her. Her duffel bag was on the ground by her feet and most of the clothes she had brought were already packed. "Stop for a minute," I grabbed her hand. She yanked it away from me and stepped back.

"Hope, what the hell is going on?" I wracked my brain, trying to think of what could have possibly happened. "We will keep you two safe, you don't need to go anywhere."

She choked out a laugh and shook her head. "Safe?" Looks like that was the wrong word to use. "Safe?" She repeated, her voice rising. "How am I supposed to trust a word that comes out of your mouth?"

I looked at her at a complete loss for words. What the fuck had happened since last night? She turned away and packed the rest of her clothes then went to step past me to the closet.

"Wait," I moved in front of her, blocking the doorway. "Please tell me what's going on," I pleaded. "Is this about the kiss?" I was grasping at straws, but none of this made any sense and my sleep deprived brain was spinning out.

"Which kiss, Jensen?" The venom there made me step back. "The one you gave me or the ones you gave Lily last night?"

I couldn't help it. I started to laugh, relief flooding me as I realized what she was upset about.

Turns out laughing was not the best way to go. Her eyes filled with tears as she growled at me, her eyes changing color to a bright blue. I stopped laughing as the aura of her wolf pressed down on mine, making him want to submit.

Before I could even process that, she tried to slip past me. I stepped to the side, blocking her again.

"Hope, wait. Please, it's not what you think."

"Really? How many fucking times can you say that and it still be true, Jensen?" She asked, her voice wavering. "I can't do this. I can't be with you, fake or not, if you're sleeping around."

"I'm not!" I said, irritation at Lily rearing up. "I have never slept with her, I promise. Please, call Sam. Call Leo. I was on the phone with one of them for most of the time I was gone, and if I wasn't with them I was in meetings. Lily was at some of the meetings, but only because she is a pack member and had to be," I pleaded, gently grabbing her hands in mine.

"I was never alone with her, let alone having sex with her."

She stared down at our hands for a minute before meeting my eyes. They had shifted back, the deep green swimming in tears.

"I can't do this," she said quietly, a tear slipping down her cheek. "It's too hard. People are getting hurt, they're fucking dying, because of me."

"No, they're dying because of Anthony." I said firmly, pulling her to me. "And we're going to stop him. Together."

She pulled back, looking at me questioningly. "You were right, Hope. The alpha's mate doesn't just sit back, whether she is an alpha or not. I shouldn't have sent you home," I said, tucking a piece of her hair behind her ear. "I'm sorry, baby."

She searched my eyes with hers, until they dropped to my lips. A bolt of heat rushed to my cock as she reached up and traced them.

"I accept your apology," She said, moving her hand down to my chest. "On one condition."

"What is it?" I asked, my breath coming out faster as she slipped her hands under my shirt.

She raised up onto her toes as she slipped her hands around my back, scratching as she went.

"I want you to fuck me. Now," she whispered in my ear, freezing me in place. She chuckled and nipped at my ear, and that was all it took.

We both started pulling at each others clothes, our desperation for each other leaving more than a few ripped things on the floor.

I pinned her to the wall, one hand playing with her nipple

while the other pulled her pants down. She threaded her hands through my hair while she panted and arched her back further.

"I want to taste you," I growled, yanking her underwear down to her pants. "Step out of these for me, love." I said, dropping to my knees to help her and smiling at how quickly she moved to listen.

"So eager," I joked, raining kisses up her thighs.

"You have no idea," she panted, smiling down at me before she pulled on my hair.

"Someone's impatient," I murmured, my cock tightening even further as she spread her legs for me. I pressed a kiss to her pussy, moaning when I felt how wet it was.

"God baby, you're always so wet for me," I groaned, licking right up her center. Her legs trembled as she moaned, threading her hands back into my hair and holding me there.

I sucked on her clit as I eased two fingers inside her. She was already tightening, her moans growing louder as she fucked my hand. I hummed as I sucked on her clit again, sending her over the edge.

"Oh god," she moaned, "Jensen, please, yes!"

"God, you are so sexy," I said, standing up and lifting her legs around my waist. She wrapped them around me, looking down and frowning when she realized I was still wearing my pants.

"Those need off. Now," she demanded as I walked her over to the bed. She knelt on it and pulled at my waistband and boxers, releasing my cock. She stared at it, her eyes heated, before leaning down and taking me into her mouth.

"Oh fuck," I ground out as I held her to me for a second. Then I pulled back, chuckling at the disappointment in her eyes.

"I wasn't done," she said, irritated.

"I know, and trust me, you're amazing at it," I said, picking her up and pinning her up further on the bed.

"The thing is," I said, raining kisses down on her neck. "If I'm going to come, I want it to be after I've been inside of you." I kissed my way down to one of her nipples, sucking it into my mouth. She gasped and arched, then wrapped her legs around me and pulled me closer.

"Is that okay with you?" I asked, raising up on to my forearms and blinking innocently. She smiled at me wickedly, lifting her hips until my cock was right at her entrance.

"More than okay," she said, grabbing my ass and pulling me into her. We both groaned as I eased inside. I took a few quick breaths, trying to let her adjust before I went pushed all the way in.

She was less patient. She pulled on me harder, pushing me in even deeper.

"Oh god," I panted, dropping my forehead to hers. "Your pussy is amazing."

"Then move," she challenged, moving her hands up to my back and digging in her nails.

My cock jumped at that and I started to move, slowly but then faster and faster as she urged me on.

"More, baby, more," she moaned, moving with me. Her pussy tightening around my cock sent me over the edge, both of us moaning for each other.

I shifted to the side so my weight wasn't on her, laying my head next to hers. She rolled over, snuggling in close, both of us spent.

We drifted off to sleep like that, holding on to each other.

# CHAPTER THIRTY-ONE

## *Hope*

There was something warm against my back. And tangled in my legs. I went to sit up and found an arm tossed over my waist, pinning me down.

I froze as memories flooded into my brain.

Jensen and I fighting.

And then..

Not fighting so much.

I felt my face warm as I thought of the things he had said, the sounds we had made. Staring up at the ceiling, I tried to think of another time that I had felt this way for someone. Anyone.

What way *was* I feeling?

Shock followed before the thought fully formed. I loved him.. I really did. Not only that, but I had always been drawn to him. Was this..

Shit.

No.

Was this what it meant to be fated mates? My wolf had wanted to bite him for years, to mark him as mine. The longer I laid there, the clearer it became.

How much I wanted to be near him, not just as a person, but as a wolf. It wasn't just because he was an alpha. It was because he was meant to be mine. And I was meant to be his.

It was all too much. Sliding out from under his arm as slowly as possible, I untangled myself from him and stood up. His hair was mussed in the back, his broad shoulders relaxed and covered in scratches that made me blush.

I pulled on new clothes from the closet and made my way downstairs.

I couldn't shake the restless energy, the knowledge that last night had changed everything. And I wasn't even remotely ready for that.

I scribbled a note about going out for a run and that I would be back by lunch, and headed out. I needed to clear my head, to let my wolf do the thinking for a little bit.

There were still guards when I went outside, and one of them stepped up to follow me.

"Nope," I said, raising a hand. "I am going alone. If you try to follow me, I will purposefully lose you."

They looked between each other, discomfort flashing across their faces.

"Tell me something, if Jensen said he didn't want guards with him, would you listen?"

"Yes," said the one closest to me, looking down.

"Exactly," I said as I drew myself up. "I'm the alpha's mate. I'm pretty sure that means my word goes as far as his." I stared at each one of them until they looked down. "So don't follow me."

I took off for a run, planning to shift once I was deeper in the woods by the river.

I could never let her out around others. God, how could an alpha be fated to someone who is too scared to let her own wolf out in public? I ran harder, the tension in my chest rising as I thought of every single thing that was wrong about this.

After ten or so minutes I made it to the river. All traces of Xander had been removed, although it smelled like someone had been there recently. Because of my pace, I was already panting a little. I moved into the trees and reached for my shirt, ready to strip before I shifted, when I heard the crack of a twig.

"Hello?"

No one answered.

"Jensen? I really need some time to myself, is that you?"

Something heavy hit the back of my head, dropping me to my knees. I turned and looked up, my eyes swimming.

I knew that face.

"Miss me honey?" My dad rasped out, stalking closer with a grin on his face. He raised his fist.

Then, there was nothing.

# CHAPTER THIRTY-TWO

## *Jensen*

I rolled over, my hand searching for Hope. My eyes popped open when it met nothing. She wasn't there. I took a deep breath, trying to remind myself that this was new to us both, she probably just needed some space.

I laid there for a minute, replaying the night. She'd been more open with me than she'd been in years and falling asleep with her in my arms had been better than I'd ever imagined. It would take time, but I knew we could do this.

This may have started off as fake, but we had been meant for each other for years. My wolf had wanted to claim her when we were 19. He had known this entire time that she was my fated mate. I got out of bed, my smile growing at the imprint she'd left on her pillow. We could do this, one day at a time.

I took a quick shower, anxious to see her. Making my way downstairs, I saw Bri going into the kitchen.

"Hey Bri, have you seen Hope?" I asked, trying to keep my voice nonchalant. She smirked as she shook her head.

"No, she left a note saying she was going for a run," she said, "whatever you two have been up to has her rattled." She sent another knowing smile my way, but I was too preoccupied to focus on it.

"A run?" I asked, worry lacing my tone. "Do you know where she went?"

"The note said she was just going down by the river. I'm pretty sure one of the guards went with her," she said reassuringly.

I hurried outside, trying to breathe through the panic blooming in my chest. Something was wrong. I could feel it, and my wolf was starting to whine.

"Lindsay," I called to the guard closest to the house. "Have you seen Hope this morning?"

She nodded, a small grimace tugging at her mouth.

"Yes," she hesitated, worry flashing through her eyes. "She said that she wanted to go for a run. Alone." My stomach lurched as I pulled out my phone, calling Sam. "I tried to tell her we couldn't do that, but she was pretty insistent. Said she would just lose us if we tried to follow her."

"It's not your fault," I told her, trying to calm mine and my wolf's mounting panic. "I'm sure she's fine." Sam's phone went to voice mail and I called again, hoping he was just sleeping.

"Hello," Sam's sleepy voice finally answered.

"Thank God. I know you're catching up on sleep, but do you know who is on guard duty by the river? Hope went down there by herself."

"Shit. Okay, I'm not sure. I'll make some calls and meet you down there," he said.

I hurried inside, grabbing my keys and heading for the car.

What's going on, Jensen?" Brianna came out into the living room, worry dancing across her face.

"It's probably nothing," I tried to keep my tone calm, but based off of how drawn she looked, I was doing a shit job. "I just want to go check on Hope. I need you to stay here, okay?"

"No, no way-" She was interrupted by Elena bursting through the front door.

"Where is she?" Elena panted, her eyes the silver of her wolf. Fear ripped through me at her question. I wasn't just imagining things, something was wrong.

"We don't know," I said tightly and turned back to Brianna. "I need you to stay here, losing track of where you are will just make it even harder for us to focus on finding her," I told her, relieved when she nodded.

"I need to talk to you," Elena bit out, her eyes still silver. She walked back outside without waiting for me to answer. I hurried after her, catching up with her in the driveway.

"He has her," she blurted as soon as I was within earshot. "He has her and they're hurting her," she swallowed and started to pace. My stomach bottomed out, pain and rage warring within me.

Lock it down, Jensen. You can't help her if you fall apart.

I took a deep breath and pulled Elena in for a hug.

"Thank you for telling me," I whispered and let her go. "Now, tell me what you saw."

# CHAPTER THIRTY-THREE

## *Hope*

"Time to wake up, princess," I tried to push at whatever was touching my face, but my hands were stuck. I hated being called princess, why would Jensen do that?

Someone was patting my cheek, softly. Then my head spun to the side as the patting became a slap. My eyes began watering, but they were too heavy to open.

"Wha- " I tried to swallow, my mouth was so dry. "What's going on?" I croaked, finally able to open my eyes a little bit.

My memory came rushing back as I took my surroundings in between slow blinks. I'd gone for a run and there had been a sound, which was the last thing I remembered.

"It's about fucking time," said a different voice, one that felt very familiar. I looked up from under my brows, recognition blasting through me.

"Dad." I bit out, dull anger spreading through me, helping me wake up. He glared down at me, disgust distorting his features.

"Took you long enough," he growled, raising his hand again. Another hand grabbed his wrist, stopping him from slapping me again.

"I told you," said Anthony in a dangerously soft voice, "That you only hit what's mine when I say you can." He stared my dad down, waiting until he broke eye contact before his attention shifted to me.

"Nice to see you conscious, princess," he drawled, "you really are not looking too good. My nephew is not treating you very well, is he?" His eyes hardened as he stared at my neck, noticing the mark there. "I see he's been busy, although I don't see any claiming marks on you."

"Fuck off," I snapped, my rage mounting.

He chuckled and motioned to someone standing behind me. My stomach dropped as I recognized who it was.

Wildwood's witch wolf.

She was looking down, her eyes hidden. I stared at the slight tremble of her hands.

She didn't want to do this.

"Have you ever heard of a blood spell?" Anthony asked, pulling my attention back to him. He had grabbed a knife and was running his fingers over the blade.

"Nope, and I'm not really interested in learning about it." I said snarkily, my eyes glued to the knife.

He chuckled, shaking his head. "You see, blood spells are exactly what they sound like. Except this one uses blood willingly given from both of us. Ellie over here," he said, nodding to the witch wolf, "came up with a really neat little spell that will keep you on pack lands. Or, at least, it'll keep you alive if you stay on pack lands. If you leave?" He asked, shrugging. "You'll die."

"What the fuck is wrong with you?" I burst out, thrilled at the irritation that flashed through his eyes.

He snapped forward, punching me in the stomach.

"Are you fucking kidding me?" I wheezed, my laughter turning to a cough. "You're delusional if you think I'm going to give you my blood. And are really going all 'if I can't have you, no one can'? You are such a fucking cliche." I laughed again, the throbbing in my ribs ratcheting up my anger even more.

He grabbed my chin, forcing me to look at him. "I may be a cliche, but I don't mind it. No one else is going to have you, especially not my fucking nephew."

"You know what's the most cliche thing about villains?" I bit out, yanking my chin out of his grip. "Someone ends them."

He laughed and turned to my dad. "Such a spicy daughter, Jason." My dad nodded, his nostrils flaring as he glared at me.

I glared back, trying to think of some way to escape. My hands were bound so tight I couldn't even move them, and they'd done the same with my legs.

I needed more time.

"Why do you even want to be my mate?" I asked. "I know that asshole is your beta," I said, nodding to my dad, "But it's not like you haven't had other mates. Why me?"

Ellie flinched at my last question, finally meeting my eyes. The sorrow and regret there shocked me. Anthony noticed where I was looking and glared at her, causing her to look down again.

"Well," he said, drawing the word out. "Did you know that magical wolves can do more than just spells?"

My thoughts immediately turned to what I'd overheard at Jensen's. "Prophecies," I whispered, shocked.

"So you do know," Anthony said, smirking. "Well, Ellie here, who is not much older than you are, had a vision when she was a child. From what I understand, they can be confusing. But one thing she learned was that one day, Wildwood and Crescent River would be united. In order for the alpha to be strong enough, his mate had to have the blood of both packs in their veins."

I couldn't shake the sense that there was something missing in that prophecy - it felt wrong.

"As you know, Wildwood and Crescent River haven't had the

easiest relationship," he continued, "And you were the only person in our entire pack who fit the bill. Well, you and your little sister."

"You mean you've been planning this?" I turned to my dad, the lack of guilt in his eyes making me feel sick. "For how long?"

"Since right before your mom died," Anthony said, his smile twisting sickeningly.

"I was," I swallowed, horrified by each new piece of information. "I was only five." Another thought followed, one almost too terrible to process.

"Did she know?" I asked, my voice wavering. My dad stared back at me in disgust.

"Did she know you were actually going to be useful?" He spat back. "Of course she fucking knew. And do you know what she did?" He stepped forward and leaned down until his face was level with mine.

"That stupid bitch tried to run."

A cold nothingness opened up inside my chest, deadening the shock I felt. I leaned forward until my nose almost touched his, channeling every bit of icy rage into my words.
"Your death won't be slow," I said softly. "I'll make sure every single nerve in your body is screaming before you find any comfort in death."

He flinched, his eyes glued to mine. I leaned back and turned my glare to Anthony, who's eyes widened slightly at the threat there. A loud yelp coming from outside startled us all, but there was nothing we could see out the window. Anthony sent a look at the man standing by the door, who immediately went outside to investigate.

# CHAPTER THIRTY-FOUR

## *Jensen*

We moved through the trees towards a small cabin.

"Are you sure this is the right spot?" I asked, my wolf pushing at my skin. He was ready to rip everyone apart. I'd been fighting with him since we found her blood after searching by the river.

"This is where Jake said the satellite showed the SUV go. There's a cabin up there that is owned by their pack, so it makes sense," Sam said reassuringly. He had been in complete shut down mode, trying to move as fast as we could to find Hope.

I nodded and looked at my brother, worry and pride overwhelming me. I hadn't wanted either of them to come with me, they were too important to our pack, but they had insisted. We'd barely been able to talk my parents and sister out of coming.

We crept farther through the woods, the lack of guards putting us on edge. As we approached the cabin, they finally came into sight. Anthony only had three guards stationed outside, two of whom were on their phones. Idiots. A hard smile spread over my face as I looked at Sam and Leo.

"What's the plan?" Leo asked, his grin matching mine.

"I want you two to draw those three away from the house. I'll get eyes inside and see who else we have to deal with."

They both nodded and moved silently through the trees to the other side of the clearing. A minute later, there was the sound of a tree branch cracking that sent all three guards scrambling towards the woods.

I crept towards the cabin, pausing underneath one of the windows. I took a deep breath, focusing on the sounds coming from inside. I could hear two men and then I felt a flood of relief. Hope. I cracked a smile as her words came through clearly.

"Your death won't be slow," she said, her rage and disdain palpable. I lifted my phone, using the camera to see into the room through the window.

There were four people I could see from that angle - Anthony, Jason, the pack's wolf who looked terrified, and another man I didn't recognize.

I heard a yelp from the woods, concern flooding me. The man I didn't recognize moved towards the door, opening it and heading towards the woods.

I looked to where I'd last seen Leo, debating on whether the yelp had come from my pack or not, when I saw Sam further away from the sound, waving me towards the cabin.

I nodded and rushed to the front door. If I moved fast enough, this could be over before they could touch Hope. I burst through the door, smiling as I launched myself at Jason.

He didn't stand a fucking chance. I tackled him and felt his claws rip across my chest, but it barely stung. He had taken my mate. He had abused her her entire life. It took everything in me to not end him then and there, but Anthony was still a threat.

I had Jason lying in a heap, barely conscious, in less than a minute. I paused as I looked around for Anthony.

"You fucking coward," I said, my voice low as I glared at him. He was standing behind Hope, his claws out and on her throat. Despite the circumstances, she was staring at me without any fear, only anger and relief.

"Take one more step and I'll end her," he said, a slight smile on his face. The woman standing next to me hadn't moved, her eyes fixed on Anthony. I heard her muttering, and Anthony was suddenly thrown backwards.

"You stupid bitch," he spat at her, popping back up to his feet. It didn't matter how fast he was, I was on him before he could step any closer to Hope.

I slammed him into the wall again, enraged. He pushed me back, his eyes starting to glow. If he shifted, it was more likely that Hope would get hurt. This cabin wasn't big enough for our wolves.

I launched myself at him again, this time taking us both to the ground. I shifted my nails into claws and held them to his throat, smiling when he froze.

# CHAPTER THIRTY-FIVE

## *Hope*

"Did you really think I would show up here with so few guards?" Anthony wheezed, blood trickling down his neck from where Jensen's claws had pierced the sides of his neck. He almost seemed... Happy.

Wait.

Fuck.

"Get out of here Jensen!" Somehow I had missed it, missed all of it. Five Wildwood Pack members flooded in, surrounding us. My father was conscious again and stood up, the rage on his face sending chills down my spine.

"You can kill me," Anthony said, raising his hands to Jensen's. "But you won't have time to stop them from killing Hope. And will someone please fucking restrain Ellie? If she uses magic again without my consent, I want you to knock her out."

My dad came over and dragged my chair to where one of the men held Ellie, smirking at Jensen as he went.

"I'll let you go if you let Hope go," Jensen said angrily, his eyes glued to mine.

"No!" I yelled, shaking my head. Anthony's pack moved in closer while my dad stayed next to me, his claws out.

"I, Jensen Valenzuela, challenge you as alpha of the Wildwood pack," he said, throwing Anthony away from him.

"That's how you're going to play this?" Anthony asked, irritated.

"Are you really going to ignore centuries of tradition?"

Anthony shook his head, a small smile on his lips. "No, I won't go against pack law," his smile grew. "But I don't have to fight you. Jason, as my beta, I order you to fight in my place."

My dad stepped toward Jensen and let loose a growl. Jensen tackled him, just missing his throat with his claws. My dad kicked Jensen off of him, wiping away the blood on his face. Jensen stepped forward again when Anthony made a small movement out of the corner of my eye.

BOOM!

The sound of a gunshot had my ears ringing, and both my dad and Jensen were lying on the ground.

I turned frantically, trying to see who had the gun, but it was already gone. Jensen was moving again, groaning as blood started to stain his shirt. Anthony stepped toward my dad, disgust across his face.

"That's two generations of Valenzuela's you've failed to kill," He said, and sliced his throat open with his claws. My brain couldn't process what I was seeing, and even though it was a gun shot wound, Jensen should be starting to heal. He tried to sit up, but his arm gave out from under him.

Anthony walked over to him and crouched down, the smile on his face growing. "I'm sure you've realized by now that that wasn't a normal bullet."

My blood turned to ice.

They used silver. He wouldn't make it unless he got out of here. Now.

"I'll do it," I said frantically, staring at Jensen. "I'll give you my blood if you let him live."

"Oh Hope," Anthony chuckled, "Why would I do that? All I have to do is leave him here to die and take you with me."

He walked towards me, leaning down to my level and putting his hand on my cheek.

"I told you that you'd be mine."

I turned towards Jensen's moan from the ground, his head raising to look at me. His eyes had been the color of his wolf's but were starting to flicker.

"Hope," he said weakly, trying again to get up. Seeing him dying on floor, with my dad's body next to him, and knowing that Anthony had won broke a dam inside of me.

All of the pain and betrayal I'd experienced flooded me until I couldn't stand it. My wolf was pushing frantically to get out, wanting so badly to shift. For once, I didn't care that I was around other people. I let her take over.

I shifted and could feel just how furious she was. Anthony and the other men in his pack stepped back to the door as I took a step forward, dwarfing them.

I could feel them trying to shift into their wolves, fighting against mine, but she was not fucking having it. Focusing on Anthony, who had shifted his eyes, I growled softly, padding towards him.

The door burst open behind them, making us all turn as Leo, Sam, Elena, and others from Crescent River darted into the room.

The room descended into chaos, and as bloodthirsty as I was, I needed to be by my mate.

My wolf hurried over to his side, pressing her nose to his cheek. His eyes opened a little as he smiled and tried to touch her face before he passed out.

# CHAPTER THIRTY-SIX

## *Jensen*

Whoever was talking so loudly really needed to shut the fuck up. The hand I lifted to cover my eyes from the light felt as if it had weights on it. A growl escaped my throat as I tried to tell whoever was being so loud to shut up.

Had I gotten drunk or something last night? What was going on -

Oh god. Hope. The cabin. The fight. I was losing!

"Jensen? Oh god, baby, please wake up. Open your eyes."

Relief flooded my veins. I'd know that voice anywhere.

"What..." I tried again, clearing my throat. "What happened?" Lifting my eyelids took as much effort as a marathon, but I managed to pry them wide enough to see Hope, my parents, and

Sam huddled next to my bed.

None of them were hurt, although they all looked exhausted. No blood was on anyone either, which was definitely not what I remembered last.

Hope and Sam exchanged a look, as if begging the other to go first.

Sam caved.

"Well. That's a really good question. Do you remember making it to the cabin?"

"Yeah, but they were waiting for us. It was a trap." My voice sounded so raspy, how many days had it been since I'd spoken?

"You're right about that. They didn't really plan for the rest of your pack to show up... I know you didn't want them to, but I had a few people ready as backup. Just in case this turned out even worse than we had planned. But by the time we fought our way into the cabin, Hope had most things under control."

"Hope had things under control? Wait..." I said, a brief memory of a massive white wolf flashing through my mind. "Did you shift? I thought they had you chained?"

"They did, but my wolf was able to break free."

"You... Hope, I could feel you. You stopped everyone else from shifting," I said, remembering how strong her wolf's will had been. "Do you have any idea what that means?"

"I didn't," she said shyly, looking at her feet. "But your parents told me." She took a steadying breath.

"I'm an alpha."

"Yeah, you are!" Sam said, laughing to himself. "Anyways, Hope saved you, pretty much kicked ass in general, and we were able to get you out."

"Wait a minute.. Did you offer to do a blood spell?" I asked, overwhelmed by the memories flooding in.

"I did," she said, biting her lip. "He was about to kill you, Jensen. And there was no way in hell I was going to lose my mate." Her eyes pierced mine, the small smile playing on her lips distracting me from what she had just said.

"Did you just call me your mate?" I asked a second later when her words had pierced the fog. I started to smile until my split lip protested. "Ow, shit. I'm sorry, are you saying what I think you're saying?"

She rolled her eyes, her hands coming to rest gently on either cheek. "Yes, you big dummy. You're my mate. I think I've always known it, and I am so sorry that almost losing you is what it took for me to admit it. I love you so much."

"Hold on," my dad said, perplexed. "I'm so lost."

"It's not the time, honey," my mom said, shaking her head at him.

"But they just said they were mates. I thought we all already knew that?"

"We did," said Sam, smirking at us. "They didn't."

# CHAPTER THIRTY-SEVEN

## *Hope*

I rolled over towards Jensen, the sun streaming in making me squint. He was staring at me, clearly much more awake than I was.

"Were you watching me sleep?" I asked, chuckling at his sheepish grin.

"Maybe," he said, looping an arm around my waist and pulling me closer. "What if I was?"

"I'd say that you should be getting more sleep, not staring creepily at your mate," I said, nuzzling into his neck.

"Creepily?" He asked, mock outrage dancing across his face as he pulled away. "It is not creepy! I dare anyone who meets you to not want to stare at you all the time," he paused, lowering his brows. "Not that they should. You're mine."

"Damn straight," I said, leaning in for a kiss. "And as much as I want to have a lazy morning, we have a lot to do."

The lighthearted tone to our morning darkened as reality crept in.

It had been three months since Anthony had abducted me and he had been missing ever since. The Wildwood Pack had a new beta who had taken over, one of his dead wives nieces, but she had been resistant to discussing anything.

"Want to go check in with everyone?" He asked, the side of his mouth quirking up. "They're probably already here to discuss the wedding."

We were also getting married next month. We'd gone back and forth about waiting until Anthony was found and dealt with, but life was too short. We'd been through too much to wait any longer.

"You're probably right," I said with a laugh. "Hopefully they brought breakfast this time, Leo is going to eat us out of house and home."

Jensen laughed and rolled out of bed, grabbing the shirt I'd thrown off of him the night before. I grabbed some new clothes from the closet and went downstairs, pausing when his phone rang from our room.

"Jensen, your phone's ringing," I called to him from the top of the stairs.

"Will you grab it?" He asked, sticking his head around the

corner. "We were right, already here. They brought donuts this time!" He said, raising his eyebrows.

I went back for his phone, chuckling until I saw who was calling.

Jake - Security was flashing across the screen. I hurried to answer it, concern and minor excitement hitting me as I wondered what news he had.

"Jake?"

"Hope? I thought I called Jensen. Never mind, it doesn't matter," he said in a rush, his anxiety creeping through the call. "There are Wildwood Pack members at the front gate. Like, a lot of them."

My eyes widened, shock punching through me. We hadn't heard from any of them in months, despite reaching out several times since the cabin. I ran down the stairs and into the kitchen, everyone pausing mid-laugh at my serious expression.

"Jake," I said as I put him on speaker phone. "How many Wildwood Pack members are at the front gate?"

"At least twenty. It looks like their new beta is there and for as far away as the camera is, I can tell that they don't look happy."

Jensen and I exchanged a look, his pleading and then resigned as I stared blandly at him. I wasn't sitting this one out for anything.

"Jensen and I will head over there now." I said shortly,

smiling at Jensen reassuringly.

"Elena, Dean, Leo, and I will be there soon too," Jenny added, raising a brow at Jensen's glare. "Don't even think about arguing with me. You and Hope may be *the* alphas, but you aren't the only alphas in our pack. And I'm your mother, so just accept it."

"I want to go too," Bri said, concern lowering her brows.

"Nope," I said firmly. "We don't know what we're walking into and you'll be safer at home."

"But -"

"Sorry Bri," Jensen said softly. "It's just not safe. We'll be back before you know it."

She stared at the two of us, irritation and affection in her eyes.

"Fine," she said grumpily. "But I won't like it."

"We wouldn't expect anything less," Jenny said with a smile as she gave her arm a soft squeeze.

We hurried out of the kitchen and into Jensen and I's SUV, all of us tense and silent on the way there. Jake was right, there were at least twenty people outside of the gate and they looked more than just irritated. More like downright pissed.

"Jensen," called one of them, a petite blond who looked barely over eighteen. "I'm the new beta for the Wildwood Pack," she paused, taking a breath. "What the fuck do you think you're doing?"

"Um, I'm sorry," he said, his amusement spilling out. "What are you? A high schooler?"

The beta blushed but kept her face straight as she waited for him to answer.

"Sorry," I said, shooting Jensen a look. "What he meant to say is what are you talking about?"

She rolled her eyes at that, shaking her head as she looked down. "I knew that this pack was full of shit, but I didn't think you were cowards, too."

"What the hell are you talking about?" Jensen asked, folding his arms and glaring at the beta.

"Our alpha, that's what I'm talking about!" She spat, her eyes shifting to blue. "We know you took him and we're here to get him back. I'll challenge you here and now if I need to."

"Woah," I said, holding up my hands. "We don't have Anthony. We'd tell everyone we'd caught him if we had, although he'd probably already be dead at that point."

She blanched at my words, her eyes darting between Jensen and I. Elena gasped quietly, and when I looked to see what was wrong she had completely stiffened. Her eyes were silver and focused on nothing as she stared straight ahead.

Jenny ran over to her and put an arm around her waist, steadying her.

"I don't know what game you're trying to play," said the beta, "but it stops right fucking now. Give us Anthony." She flinched as Jensen turned to her, his eyes full of fire.

"We don't fucking have him," he said quietly, his tone deadly. "If we did, I would give you his head because that's all that would be left of him. Now, if you'll excuse us, something is wrong with my sister."

Jensen pulled out his phone and called Sam, requesting back up to the perimeter. I hurried over to Elena, grabbing her hand right before she relaxed and almost fell over. Her eyes faded back to their natural blue, her face pale. She shook her head and turned to me with fear flooding her face.

"We need to get back to your house. Now." She said, starting to shake.

"What did you see Lena?" Dean asked quietly, guiding her back to the car.

"It can wait. We need to get back to Brianna. Now," she said urgently, her hands still quivering.

We all rushed into the car at the mention of Brianna and Jensen took off when the last door closed. I called Sam and asked him to meet us there, telling him the bare minimum but that something could be wrong.

The house looked normal when we pulled up, with Sam pulling in right behind us.

"Where's the guard?" Leo asked, making my stomach drop. I'd forgotten someone was supposed to be on patrol at our house still. Whoever it was supposed to be, they weren't around right now.

I jumped out of the car and raced inside, barely aware of the footsteps behind me.

"Bri?" I called as soon as I passed through the front door. "Bri!"

"Hope," Jensen said, his tone making my heart stop. I ran to where he was standing at the top of the stairs, his eyes glued to the corner above the stair rail. The corner that should be white but was now smeared with red. Red in the shape of a hand print.

"There's a note!" Jenny called from the kitchen, her voice wavering. Jensen pulled me away from the stairs and into the kitchen.

"It says," Jenny paused, taking a deep breath as her hand holding the note shook. "It says 'I'll settle for Brianna if it means I can have both packs. Turn over leadership of your pack or I'll make sure she suffers every day for the rest of her life.'" She looked up at me, hesitating before she added.

"It's signed by Anthony."

## Thank You

I hope you enjoyed The Alpha Pair! Next up in The Blood Pack Prophecy Series is The Beta Pair, which releases in May 2023.

I'd like to invite you to sign up for my PNR After Dark Book Club. You'll get emails about new releases, bonus scenes, and giveaways. If emails aren't your thing, join me on TikTok @author.nicolerivers

Thank you so much for reading!

## About Nicole

*Author Nicole Rivers*

Nicole Rivers lives in Alaska with her partner and three kids. Yes, it really is *that* cold sometimes, but the sun is up all summer - which makes up for it. She can be found muttering over her husband's laptop (it writes better), planting too many seeds for her garden, or being climbed on by no less than two tiny humans.

Printed in Great Britain
by Amazon

37571553R00121